⋆ A Bliss Bakery Story ⋆

SWEET

Kathryn Littlewood

HarperCollins *Children's Books*

First published in paperback in Great Britain by HarperCollins
Children's Books in 2013
HarperCollins *Children's Books* is a division of HarperCollins*Publishers* Ltd,
77-85 Fulham Palace Road, Hammersmith, London, W6 8JB.

www.harpercollins.co.uk

1

Copyright © 2013 by The Inkhouse

ISBN 978-0-00-745176-0

For my beloved Grampy,
a craftsman of the highest order

Contents

Prologue

PREPACKAGED MAGIC

IT WAS NINE months after her Aunt Lily stole the Bliss Cookery Booke right out from under her nose that Rosemary Bliss discovered something horrible on the shelves of Ralph's Supermarket in downtown Calamity Falls.

Rose's sneakers squeaked on the floor as she stopped dead in her tracks.

Staring back at her from the front of each of dozens of cardboard boxes was the smiling face of her lying, conniving aunt. Each box bore a banner reading LILY'S MAGIC INGREDIENT! AS SEEN ON TV.

The economy-sized tub of mayonnaise Rose had been carrying slipped from her fingers and fell to its death on the floor. "Mum!" she cried.

Rose's mother, Purdy, ran over. "Oh dear."

"No, Mum, not the mayonnaise. Look!" Rose pointed at the boxes of Lily's Magic Ingredient.

Since she'd disappeared with the Bliss family's magical Cookery Booke, Aunt Lily had made good on her promise to use it to become famous. She had written a bestselling cookbook, *Lily's 30-Minute Magic*, and had a cooking show on TV. Now there she was, smiling happily on the shelves of their very own supermarket, while the rest of Calamity Falls had fallen into a grim malaise.

Without the Booke, Purdy and Albert Bliss had no choice but to make ordinary pies and muffins and croissants from the pages of an ordinary Betty Crocker cookbook. The baked goods were still delicious, of course, and the residents of Calamity Falls still came by every morning as they always had; but the magic of the town had dried out, leaving everything and everyone in it feeling a bit like warm lettuce: sickly, grey, and wilted.

In the picture on the box, Lily looked as beautiful as ever. She had grown out her close-cropped hair, and now it fell to her shoulders in perfectly wavy heaps the colour of black chocolate. She was smiling seductively, her hands covered with orange oven mitts and planted on her hips. "Add a tablespoon to any of

Lily's 30-Minute Magic recipes," the box read, "for a dash of *magic!*"

"Listen to this!" cried Purdy, reading from the box. "'Not a sufficient source of Iron or Vitamin C. Ingredients: Secret. FDA approval pending.'"

"Why would anyone eat anything that hadn't been approved by the FDA?" Rose asked.

"Lily is a celebrity," Purdy said, brushing her wild bangs from her eyes. "People see her face, and they plunk down a credit card. Plus, look at the size of this fine print."

FDA APPROVAL PENDING.

"What do we do, Mum?" Rose whispered, the hairs on the back of her neck standing as straight as soldiers. Rose already felt guilty enough knowing that the biggest mistake of her young life – trusting her treacherous aunt Lily – had brought calamity to Calamity Falls. The thought that the calamity had spread to the rest of the world was just too much guilt to bear.

"What we do is figure out exactly what this 'magic ingredient' is," Purdy said, rolling up the sleeves of her tattered blue coat. She swept box after box into her red plastic shopping cart until the shelf was empty.

*   *   *

Rose and her mother spent the rest of the weekend baking all of the recipes from *Lily's 30-Minute Magic* and adding a dash of Lily's Magic Ingredient to each one.

The Magic Ingredient was a blueish-grey powder that smelled like burned toast. When Rose threw a tablespoon of the Magic Ingredient into the batter for Lily's Gooey Chocolate Pudding Cake, the batter sizzled like hot oil and whispered her aunt's name with each pop: "*Liiiilllllyyyyy!*"

When Rose tossed a tablespoon into the crust of Lily's Caramel Apple Tarte Tatin, the crust rattled on the table, giggling "*Lily!*"

The same happened with the Lily's Vanilla Bean Crème Brûlée, the Cherry Clafouti à la Lily, and the Just Peachy Peach Pie.

Rose's brothers, Ty and Sage, walked through the kitchen on their way to play basketball in the driveway. "Did someone say 'Lily'?" Ty asked. In the time since the Bliss Cookery Booke had been stolen, Ty had grown taller still. He gelled his red hair straight up in the front so that it looked like he was wearing a tiara two inches high, or a tiny, red-picket fence. He had treated himself to a bottle of cologne from the pharmacy for his sixteenth birthday, and he smelled like a walking European discotheque.

"I thought we weren't allowed to say her name!" Sage cried into his portable tape recorder. Rose's younger brother had read that some stand-up comedians recorded themselves in normal conversation in case anything funny came out, and so he'd started recording every comment he uttered in case he later needed the material for a stand-up routine. Sage had grown taller as well, and his cheeks had grown proportionally puffier, as had the red curls atop his head.

"No one said her name," Purdy replied.

"I was just telling Mum about my new friend, Tilly," Rose said. "And my other friends Billy and Gilly. . . who live in Philly."

Ty and Sage squinted suspiciously at their sister and their mother, then scooted outside.

Rose and Purdy continued their dreadful experiment. Lily's Low-Fat Pound-for-Pound Cake came out of the oven smelling like burned rubber, as did the Deep-Fried Cookie Dough Balls, the Luscious Lemon Squares, and Lily's Bodacious Brioche Bread Pudding.

"Are we overcooking them?" Rose asked.

"No!" her mother exclaimed, confused. "If anything, we're undercooking them!"

By the time Rose and Purdy were finished, every

surface of the Follow Your Bliss Bakery kitchen was covered with plates of cakes, cookies, pies, and puddings, each containing a tablespoon of Lily's Magic Ingredient. The kitchen itself was filled with a subtle, acrid, sinister smell.

"How do we find out if they're dangerous?" Rose asked.

Purdy brushed flour from the wild curls of her hair. "I don't know," she admitted. "Do we dare try them ourselves?"

As Rose pondered what to do with the potentially poisonous baked goods, Purdy clicked on the portable TV that the family kept atop the counter in case of emergencies.

Much to Rose's dismay, Aunt Lily appeared on the screen, wearing a fitted black cocktail dress. They had happened to tune in to her cooking show. "Here it is, folks – the world's best devil's food cake!" Lily said. "And you know what that means: Time for the C-word!"

She raised her arms like a preacher while the live studio audience chanted wildly, "Chocolate! Chocolate! Chocolate!"

Rose changed the channel in disgust, then wiped the flour-ridden remote control on her jeans. A commercial popped on.

"Now for a limited time only, Lily's Special Spatulas are only nineteen dollars and ninety-five cents! Order today and we'll include a Bombastic Bundt Pan, absolutely free!"

Rose changed the channel again. "Jeez louise!"

Lily again. This time she was on the set of a talk show, wearing a different fitted black cocktail dress. "The secret to my success?" she said, coyly batting her eyelashes. "Why, my passion for baking, of course!"

"Turn on the news!" Purdy yelled, and Rose changed the channel yet again.

"In entertainment today," said the newsreader, "a new record has been broken: *Lily's 30-Minute Magic* has become the highest-rated daytime cooking show in the history of television broadcasting. Its ratings have actually exceeded the number of televisions in America, a statistic that continues to baffle authorities."

Rose and Purdy were busy ogling the television screen when Leigh waddled into the kitchen. "I want lunch, Mummy."

"Lunch is in half an hour, Leigh." Without looking down, Purdy reached a hand to tousle Leigh's head. "I see you've had a haircut." Since she'd turned four, Leigh had insisted on cutting her own hair. This resulted in a mop of shaggy black chunks of every conceivable length. "Why don't you go get your bow, and I'll tie up your hair."

"Okay!" Leigh said, and turned to go.

But she didn't go far. Mesmerised by the Lily-a-thon on the TV, Rose and her mother didn't notice as Leigh reached atop the counter and gobbled down the entirety of Lily's foot-long Pound-for-Pound Cake.

Leigh sat on the ground for a minute, licked her fingers, then stood and cleared her throat.

"Wow, that's tremendous!" she said in a voice far too deep and gravelly and sophisticated to be coming from such small lips. "That was just a tremendous pound cake. So sweet – but not cloyingly so; velvety, rich, moist. . . Who is responsible for this confectionary delight?"

Rose and Purdy spun around and stared at the little girl, who, a moment before, had hardly known what a pound cake was, let alone the meaning of the word *cloyingly*.

Oh no, Rose thought.

Leigh looked up at the TV and saw Lily sitting on the set of the news show, her long, tanned legs crossed. "Of course! It's Lily, of *Lily's 30-Minute Magic*, hostess of the most highly-rated television programme in American history! Lily, the doyenne of Danish, the priestess of parfait, the grande dame of graham crackers! It's a shame that her charisma should be confined to the realm of baking – she should run for public office!" Leigh stopped a moment, savouring this new idea. "Yes! Lily should be the first female president of the United States! She's the centaur of cinnamon buns! The sultan of—"

Purdy clapped a hand over Leigh's mouth and looked at Rose in horror.

Leigh's irises had widened so much that her pupils were an endless vortex of shimmering black.

Rose sank into the red-leather booth of the dining table, stunned. "If Lily gets people to eat this mix," Rose said gravely, "she'll have the country in the palm of her hand." Rose pulled the worn fleece hood of her green sweatshirt over her eyes. Not only did Lily want fame, but now it seemed she wanted power, too.

Leigh broke loose from Purdy's grip and marched towards the back door. "I'll not be chained like chattel! I'm off to find Lily and tell her how magnificent she is in person!" She shut the back door behind her, leaving Rose and Purdy among the mess of pans and tainted baked goods, sweaty and covered with flour and splatters of yellow batter.

"Our first order of business," said Purdy, "is to turn Leigh back to normal. Then we clean this kitchen. And then—"

But Rose didn't need to be told what the third order of business was. The country was in serious danger, and it was all Rose's fault. She didn't know how she was going to do it, but she knew she would have to steal back the Bliss Cookery Booke.

Chapter 1

THE CHALLENGE WILL BE TELEVISED

LILY BALANCED PRECARIOUSLY on a pair of high-heeled shoes as she pulled a tray of steaming pumpkin muffins from the convection oven in the wall of her studio kitchen. She turned to the audience and displayed the muffins, which looked slightly out of place in the hands of a woman wearing a short black cocktail dress and five-inch stilettos. "Have you ever seen anything more gorgeous in your life?"

Lily set the tray down on the countertop and raised both her arms. "Can you smell it, folks?"

Everyone in the audience hopped to their feet and chorused, "Cinnamon! Cinnamon! Cinnamon!"

Everyone, that is, except for Rose and Ty.

"Cheater! Cheater! Cheater!" Rose whispered to her

older brother as they sank down into their back-row seats.

Lily's studio kitchen had bright yellow walls, sunny orange cabinets, and an island in the centre covered with turquoise tiles. A window in the back of the kitchen opened on to a New York City skyline.

Fake, Rose thought, her fists clenched. *Just like her. This studio's in Connecticut!*

Rose looked out at the rows and rows of giddy audience members, at the hundreds of bright lights hanging from a grid on the ceiling above, and at the cameras, five in total. Rose tried to imagine how important Lily must feel standing in front of all those doting eyes, and the millions more watching at home. So *this* was the glamour that Rose had turned down when she told Aunt Lily that she wouldn't be going with her to New York.

Rose knew she'd made the right decision. If she'd gone with Lily, her family would right now be sitting around the kitchen table, sensing that something was missing but with no memory that Rose or the Booke had ever existed. Rose would never be able to see them again, not even in a photograph. No amount of fame or acclaim was worth losing the love of her family.

And yet, where had love gotten the Blisses? These days the streets of Calamity Falls felt cold and grey, even in the springtime. Mrs Havegood's fibs had become far less inventive, the League of Lady Librarians had retired their tour bus, and Mr Bastable and Mrs Thistle-Bastable had lost their burning passion for each other. There was no laughter, no magic. The soul of Calamity Falls had shrivelled like a dead leaf, and it was all her fault.

Even Devin Stetson had lost his lustre. Since Lily had stolen the book, Rose had worked up the courage to speak to Devin Stetson on five separate occasions, about two things: twice in the hallway about the difficulty of algebra, twice at the counter of Stetson's Doughnuts and Automotive Repair about the difficulty of algebra again, and once at the counter of the Bliss Bakery.

"How are you?" she'd said, her right eye twitching nervously, as it always did in his presence.

"Oh, fine, I guess." Devin sighed. His floppy bangs, formerly the colour of spun gold, were now just pale, dull blond. "The Calamity Falls Community Chorus disbanded. No one felt like singing any more."

"I'm sorry," Rose had replied. She had wanted to reach

out and touch his sullen cheek, but she was too afraid, and too guilty.

Rose sighed at the memory, and glared out at Lily. As much as Rose hated her aunt, the person she was most angry with was herself. If she had just been a little wiser, if she hadn't trusted Aunt Lily and fallen for her flattery, everyone she loved in her town would be happy and healthy. But as it stood, every time Rose traipsed down the grey streets of Calamity Falls, she was reminded of the grim mess she'd caused.

"This beard itches," Ty whined, tugging at the long, grey beard their father, Albert, had glued to his face hours before. "And the beard glue smells like a chemical-processing plant. I might pass out." Ty shifted in his white linen robe. "Why did I have to wear the skirt?"

"It'll be over soon," Rose said, patting him on the shoulder. "I'm pretty sure the Question-and-Answer portion is next."

Rose spoke as calmly as she could, but her hands were shaking. Appearing on television for the first time was nerve-racking enough, but Rose was about to appear on television for the first time and do something crazy.

"OK, sit, sit!" Lily called. "Let's move on to Question-and-Answer. And while we do, I'm going to dig into one of these Pump-Me-Up Pumpkin Muffins – if you all don't mind. All this talk of cinnamon has me very hungry."

She winked coyly as she unwrapped the accordion of aluminium foil from the bottom half of one of the hot muffins and sank her gleaming teeth in. She wiped the corner of her mouth. There was never a crumb on Lily's lip, never a hair out of place. She was perfection.

Rose knew this was her chance to strike. She raised her hand high and waved it back and forth until Lily noticed her in the back row. "You, sweet thing in the back with the blonde curls!"

Ty wasn't the only one wearing a disguise. Rose had pulled back her long, black hair and pinned it under a wig of blonde ringlets that Purdy had bought at the Halloween Haven in Calamity Falls. Rose was wearing a dress of pale-blue satin with poofy sleeves and an even poofier skirt that sat atop layer after layer of itchy blue crinoline.

"Are the disguises really necessary?" Rose had asked her mother before they'd left for the studio. "If I had a shepherd's staff, I would look just like Little Bo Peep."

"You'll need the disguises to ask your question," Purdy had warned her. "If Lily recognises you, she'll never call on you."

A bearded man with a headset handed Rose a microphone as Rose stood. It took all her strength not to collapse. This was the moment of truth.

Rose raised the microphone to her trembling lips and spoke in a whisper. "Testing? Testing?" The microphone squealed with feedback.

"The microphones work!" Lily said. She was chuckling, but her eyes were narrowed. It was the same look of impatience that Rose had seen on her aunt's face those times in the Bliss Bakery kitchen, the same look that Rose had chosen to ignore.

Look where ignoring my instincts has gotten me, Rose thought. *Wearing a wig on TV.*

But Rose knew – and her family agreed – that this was the only way to right the wrong that had been done.

Rose cleared her throat. "I think your Pump-Me-Up Pumpkin Muffins are bland and dry," Rose said, pushing the words past the arid bubble of fear that squatted in her throat. She took a deep breath. "*I could make a better pumpkin muffin.*"

Everyone in the audience gasped and turned to look at her.

Lily glared at Rose. Then, for just an instant, Lily's

eyes went wide, and Rose knew that Lily had recognised her.

"Ha! We have a comedian in the audience!" Lily said, giggling and clapping. "That's so cute! Next question!"

Before the next person could stand, Ty bounded up from his seat and pointed a finger in the air. In his grey beard and red cloak, he looked like Santa Claus. "This young lady, whom I have never seen before and am not related to, deserves a chance to bake!"

The studio fell silent. Scattered applause fluttered up from the audience.

Rose raised the microphone once more. "I challenge you, Lily Le Fay, to compete against me in the Gala des Gâteaux Grands in Paris, France."

Rose handed the microphone back to the young man with the headset and plopped into her seat, her arms folded across her chest.

The audience gasped once more, looking back and forth between their idol and the curly-haired little girl who had just challenged her to a duel at the world's most prestigious televised pastry competition – back and forth, back and forth, like they were watching a tennis match.

Lily stood frozen in the centre of her studio kitchen,

wobbling on the points of her high-heeled shoes. Lily had no choice but to accept the challenge. If she didn't, it would look like she was afraid of being outdone by an adolescent.

Suddenly Lily's face transformed, her glare replaced by a sweet smile. "I accept the challenge! I will compete against this brave young thing at the Gala des Gâteaux Grands!"

The audience went wild, clapping and hooting and hollering.

"What's your name, sweetheart?" Lily asked.

Rose stood and pulled off the blonde wig, letting her long, black hair cascade down to her shoulders. "My name is Rosemary," she said. "Rosemary Bliss."

Beside her, Ty discreetly pumped his fist. *"Yes!"* he said.

"Well, *Rosemary Bliss.*" Lily spat out the name as if it were another term for a skin disease. "Just because you're little doesn't mean I'm going to go easy on you. You know that, right?"

"Yup," Rose said defiantly. And she curtsied to her Aunt Lily, who steadied herself by leaning up against the kitchen counter.

I can't believe I just did that, thought Rose.

*   *   *

At the end of the show, while the rest of the audience was filing out, the bearded man in the headset plucked Rose and Ty from the line. "Lily wants to see both of you," he said. "This is huge! She never wants to see anyone!

"I'm Bruno," he went on, leading Rose and Ty down a back hallway of the studio. "But Lily still doesn't know my name. She calls me Bill. But hey, she's Lily! She could call me Armpit for all I care."

Rose scowled. It seemed Lily had everyone in the country wrapped around her elegant pinkie finger.

At the end of the hall was a metal door painted blue, with a sign in the shape of a star that read MS LE FAY.

Bruno knocked quietly on the door. "I have the little girl and the old man here, Lily!"

"Oh, thanks, Bill!" she called. "Send them in!"

Bruno pulled the door open, and Rose and Ty walked into what could only be described as a palace. In the centre of the room gushed a stone fountain ringed by ornate cast-iron benches. A lush forest of orchids hung from the ceiling, and flowing swathes of blue silk draped the walls.

And there, sitting in a hammock, rocking gently from side to side, was Lily. She was wearing a plush white

27

robe, like she'd just emerged from the shower; only her perfect black hair was dry. Even in a bathrobe, she looked ready for an awards show.

"Have a seat by the fountain, Rosemary. You, too, Thyme."

Rose sat with her brother on one of the cast-iron benches and looked up at the massive fountain, which was a fifteen-foot marble statue of Lily stirring a spoon around an overflowing bowl, her neck long and elegant.

"It's so nice to see both of you again! How do you like my little dressing room?" Lily stepped out of the hammock.

"I gotta say, it's pretty sweet, *Tia* Lily," Ty said, looking around.

Lily perched on the edge of the fountain, folding one tanned, silky leg over the other. "Let's get down to business. Your little stunt today was reckless, to say the least. What exactly are you trying to do?"

Rose sat up straight and cleared her throat. "Losing the Gala des Gâteaux Grands would ruin you. But unlike you, I don't have a reputation to worry about. I'm *twelve*. So we're offering you a deal. I will lose the competition on purpose if you just give us back our Cookery Booke and stop selling Lily's Magic Ingredient."

Lily feigned surprise. "Right, the Booke! You want the *Booke* back. Of course. I'd forgotten all about it."

"You already have a TV show, *Tia* Lily," said Ty. "What do you still need the Booke for? Our town is in trouble!"

Lily plucked a bit of fuzz off her white robe and flicked it into the fountain. "See, this is the problem with the Bliss family. None of you has any ambition. You're more concerned with your Podunk town than with succeeding. You think that just because I host the highest-rated daytime TV show in history and have a fifteen-foot marble statue of myself in my enchanted-forest-themed dressing room that I have 'enough.' There is never enough!"

Lily stood and sauntered towards the brilliantly lit mirror on her make-up table. "I could have *real* power. I could be running the country! But I can't do it without the Booke. Or Lily's Magic Ingredient."

Ty itched under his beard. "Wow, *Tia* Lily. You're scary. You're like a devil-aunt. You're like. . . a *tia*. . . but you're also the Devil, *El Diablo*. You're like. . . *El Tiablo!*"

"So, you see, I can't give it back in exchange for you throwing the contest," said Lily as she examined her flawless cheek in the mirror, hunting for clogged pores that weren't there. "And I can't stop selling Lily's Magic Ingredient."

"But—" Rose began to protest just as two men wearing suit jackets and polo shirts burst through the door.

"There you are, you geniuses!" said the shorter of the two. The taller one was studying the screen on his mobile phone.

"My name is Joel," said the short one. "I'm one of the producers of *Lily's 30-Minute Magic*. This is our other producer, Kyle."

The taller man looked up from his mobile phone for a moment and nodded, then looked back down.

Joel shook Rose's hand. "You were fabulous today," he said enthusiastically. "I thought maybe Kyle had arranged your showdown with Lily as a birthday present to me, but he was as surprised as I was!"

Rose gave a confused half smile.

"Anyway, we can't wait for this year's Gala des Gâteaux Grands," Joel said. "Could a twelve-year-old girl possibly beat Lily Le Fay, the world's most famous baker? It's genius! Everyone in the universe will be tuning in to watch! And that includes aliens!

"We'll get all the contracts ironed out later," Joel went on. "For now, just know that you've made us very happy producers. Kisses!" he said, kissing the air on either side of Rose's cheek.

"Bye," muttered Kyle.

After Joel and Kyle had closed the dressing room door behind them, Lily went back to examining her skin in the mirror. "As I was saying, I can't just give the Booke back, or stop selling Lily's Magic Ingredient. But I also can't back down from your challenge, because I already accepted on TV. That would make me look like a chump. Am I a chump? I don't think so. Do chumps wear plush cotton robes and smell like lilacs? No. The only way to settle this is to play it out at the Gala fair and square."

"You mean," Rose said, wincing, "actually compete?"

"Yes, actually compete! Did you think I would just roll over without a fight?" Lily swung around on her dressing stool to face Rose and Ty. "If you win, which you won't, I'll stop selling Lily's Magic Ingredient, and I'll give you back the Booke, and you can continue to lock it in a closet in your refrigerator and let its power go to waste. But if I win – and I *will* win – you'll swear to me that not a single member of your scraggly, weird, classless family will ever come near me or the Booke again."

Rose gulped. Now, if she lost the Gala des Gâteaux Grands to Lily, she would lose the Booke forever.

"Don't worry, *Tiablo*. Rosita's gonna bring it. Hard." Ty patted Rose on the back. "But how do we know you're not lying? What's to stop you from holding on to the Booke or making more Magic Ingredient after you lose?"

Now Rose patted her brother on the back. She hadn't even thought of that.

"Come with me," said Lily.

Rose and Ty followed Lily out of her dressing palace and on to the set of *Lily's 30-Minute Magic*.

Rose looked out at the rows and rows of empty seats, at the darkened grid of lights hanging from the ceiling. The studio was cold without all those giddy fans.

Lily set to work, tossing some pantry ingredients into a metal mixing bowl: flour, brown sugar, eggs, butter, milk.

"What are you making?" Rose asked.

"I am making a No-Renege Rugelach," Lily said, twirling the spoon through the batter. "After eating one of these, neither of us will be capable of going back on our word."

Lily unlocked a small drawer beneath the sink of her TV kitchen and pulled out a miniature blue mason jar filled with a clear, viscous liquid.

"And what is that goop you're putting in?" Ty asked.

"Throughout the ages, the majestic ring fairies have been known for never going back on their word. This," Lily said, pouring a few drops of the clear gloop over the rest of the ingredients, "is their saliva."

"*Great*," said Ty, rolling his eyes.

Thirty minutes later, Lily pulled the tray of No-Renege Rugelach from the oven and handed Rose and Ty two piping-hot pieces. "On three, we eat," Lily said, lifting a piece herself. "One. . . two. . . three."

Rose shifted the flaky, buttery roll of dough from one set of burned fingertips to the other, back and forth. She never imagined actually having to beat Lily at the Gala des Gâteaux Grands. She had no idea how – or even if – she could win.

"Well?" asked Lily, popping the rugelach in her mouth. "Are you going to eat it or not?"

At that moment, Rose hated her aunt so thoroughly that she felt her blood get hot. *I can beat her,* she thought. *I have to.*

She stuffed the rugelach into her mouth and swallowed.

Exhausted, Rose and Ty stumbled out the back door of the studio to find Purdy and Albert there to greet them. Sage and Leigh were seat-belted in the back of the Bliss family van.

"How did it go?" Purdy asked, kneeling on the sidewalk. She was wearing the same filthy, striped apron that she wore every day, which looked right at home in the Bliss kitchen but seemed very out of place next to a television studio.

"She accepted," said Rose.

"She'll do the contest?" asked Purdy.

Rose nodded.

"And you'll lose on purpose, and she'll give back the cookbook?" Purdy asked.

"No," said Rose.

Albert paused nervously. "What do you mean, no? Wasn't that the plan?" Since losing the Cookery Booke, he had stopped shaving, as well as exercising. His cheeks had filled out considerably, and a thick beard the texture of steel wool had enveloped the lower half of his face.

Rose gulped. "She said she'll give back the Booke if we beat her fair and square. And if we lose, we have to promise never to go looking for it again. It's lost forever."

"Oh," said Purdy quietly. "That's another matter entirely, isn't it."

"Yup!" Albert shouted, beginning to hyperventilate. "Oh boy!"

Rose hung her head. "I'm sorry. I don't know how it went wrong. I was sure she'd give the Booke back if I offered to throw the contest! But now I actually have to beat her! And we ate a No-Renege Rugelach, so there's no backing down now."

Purdy cupped Rose's cheek in her hand. "Well, you know what this means."

"What?"

"You're going to have to win the Gala des Gâteaux Grands."

Rose hung her head.

"Oh boy," Albert repeated, pacing around the concrete sidewalk, scratching at his sweaty, round head.

"Albert, love, you're not helping," Purdy said. "Don't worry, Rose. You don't have to do it alone. We're all going to beat Lily together. We'll be with you every step of the way."

Leigh called out to Rose from her car seat in the back of the van. "Foolish, simple Rose!" She chuckled. "Daring to duel with the mistress of muffins!"

"You *have* to win," Purdy continued, "if only so that we can get our hands on the recipe for Turn-Back Trifle and fix our little Lily-loving monster here. I'm assuming the effects of Lily's Magic Ingredient wear off shortly if you just eat a little bit of it, but Leigh ate a whole pound cake. She could be stuck like this forever if we don't get the Booke back."

Leigh folded her arms across her dirty *101 Dalmatians* T-shirt. "Oh, Purdy!" she called. "My bladder is. . . replete. If we don't get to a bathroom soon, we're going to have a situation on our hands!"

Purdy rolled her eyes. "Come on," she said, loading Rose and Ty into the van. "We only have five days before we have to fly to Paris for the competition."

"Good," said Sage. "I forgot my blue pyjama trousers at home. I have to get them."

"Sorry, Sage, but we're not going back to Calamity Falls," said Purdy. "We are going to Mexico. We need to pick up your great-great-great-grandfather Balthazar Bliss."

Albert settled in the driver's seat and turned the key while the van sputtered into gear.

"We have a great-great-great-grandfather?" Sage asked, brandishing his tape recorder. "Is he a mummy?"

"No, not yet," Purdy replied. "He's very spry. We need to see him because he has a second copy of the Booke.

Unfortunately, Balthazar's copy is written in another language, and he's the only one left in the world who speaks it. He's been working on a translation, but he's slow. When last we checked, he'd only managed to translate six of the seven hundred and thirty-two recipes."

"We need him to hurry it up," said Ty.

"No time for that. We're going to need his help." Purdy grimaced. "Unfortunately."

"Why 'unfortunately'?" Rose asked.

Purdy sighed. "You'll see."

Chapter 2

A CAT OF MANY WORDS

THE DUSTY MAIN road of the village of Llano Grande cut through a lush green mountain. As the Bliss van rumbled over the dirt, Ty and Sage dozed in the backseat, while Leigh muttered long sentences to herself that no one but she understood.

They'd driven for two days straight, all to get a copy of the Booke. Suddenly an obvious solution occurred to Rose. "Mum," she asked, "why didn't you guys ever make a *photocopy* of the Booke? Just so you'd have an extra?"

"The Booke can't be photocopied," Albert replied, turning the wheel with one hand and fanning his face with the other. "You put it on a copy machine, the pages come out blank. It's an odd trick of the Booke. Can't be photographed, either. Remember that picture in the newspaper of your mum baking Love Muffins?"

When the photo was taken, the Booke had been sitting open on the chopping block, where it often sat. But in the picture, there was no Booke – only an empty countertop.

"The Booke knows how to protect itself. The only way to duplicate it is to copy it by hand," he said. "And your mother and I were always too busy. Plus, that would have meant one more copy of the Booke floating around that we had to protect. Bad enough a copy fell into Lily's hands." Albert hushed his voice and turned to Purdy. "Imagine if another copy got to. . . you-know-who?"

"Who?" Rose cried.

"Let's just say," said Purdy, "that there are far worse bakers in the world than Lily Le Fay."

"Anyway," Albert went on, "you can't even take the Booke apart. Once you remove a page, the recipe goes haywire. There is magic in the Cookery Booke binding that keeps everything in working order. That's why there are only two copies in the world."

A minute later, Albert pulled off the main road and rolled to a stop near a brick hut with an overhanging tin roof. Leather saddles and empty canteens dangled from the sides of the roof, and the front porch was littered with sacks of corn and stacks of firewood. A sign hung from the tin roof: LA PANADERÍA BLISS.

"We're here!" said Purdy, swallowing hard. "Everybody just be nice to him and we'll all make it out alive."

Rose touched her finger to the screen door of La Panadería Bliss, and it creaked open. Albert and Purdy stood behind her, with Sage and Ty and Leigh heading up the rear.

It was dusty and dark inside. An empty hostess stand sat next to the door.

Ty glanced back up at the sign. "What's a *panadería?*" he whispered.

"A bakery," Albert whispered back.

"This doesn't look like a bakery," Ty said.

He's right, thought Rose. There were no tables, no chairs, no glass counter top, and no baked goods. It was a tiny, stuffy, windowless room with a damp floor and a toppled stack of chairs in the corner.

"Oh dear," Purdy mumbled. "He's probably gone off to a nursing home. I can't blame him – I mean, he is one hundred and twenty-seven years old."

Rose noticed a little silver bell sitting on top of the

hostess stand. She reached out and pressed her palm against it.

Leigh balled her tiny hands into fists and crossed her arms. "And I suppose it would have killed you to call ahead? Lily, the empress of empanadas, would have called ahead."

"Well, Lily isn't your mother, now is she?" Purdy said.

Just then a tall man with a thick chest and shrivelled, spindly limbs hustled through a doorway in the back of the dingy room. His head was mostly bald except for two patches of grey above his ears. He wore spectacles and a sour frown.

"*Hola*," he grumbled, grabbing six menus from the hostess stand. "Follow me."

"Great-great-grandfather Balthazar?" Purdy ventured. "It's me, Purdy."

"Who?" Balthazar asked.

"Purdita Bliss, your great-great-granddaughter. We called about the translation of your copy of the Bliss Cookery Booke. Remember?"

"I wish you all could just drop all the 'greats' and call me *Grandpa*. Makes a fellow feel old." Balthazar squinted at Purdy for a moment, then half-heartedly took Purdy's hand and shook it. "Oh, now I remember,"

he said. "The people with the son named after a spice."
Balthazar squinted at Ty's crown of gelled red hair that
stood two inches high. "What does he think he is, a
hedgehog?"

"That's Ty!" Albert stepped forward and shook
Balthazar's hand. "And these are the rest of our children,
Parsley, Sage, and Rosemary."

Balthazar nodded, still frowning. "More herbs. Huh."

"Is this the bakery?" Rose ventured.

"Of course not." Balthazar grunted. "This is the grand
entrance. The bakery is this way."

Balthazar led the Bliss clan through the back door on
to a noisy, sunny patio crowded with picnic tables.
Dozens of tanned Mexican farmers and their children
were sitting at the tables, laughing as they gobbled
slices of moist cake and brilliant red pie from paper
plates.

"*This* is the bakery."

Rose noticed a young woman and a young man
sitting across from each other at a table, both eating
some sort of goopy yellow mush from white bowls.
Rose stared at it, furrowing her eyebrows in confusion.
What is that stuff doing in a bakery? she wondered.

"What?" said Balthazar crankily. "You don't like the look of my polenta, Marjoram?"

"It's Rosemary," Rose mumbled.

"Whatever, Marjoram. Come to my office. All of you."

Balthazar led the Blisses to a tin shed at the back of the patio. Inside was a shady room with an odd concrete structure in the centre. The structure was shaped like an Olympic podium, with two lower platforms flanking one high column. At the top of the column was a grate, and beneath it roared a wood fire.

"My stove," the old man grumbled. "I know it's not one of your high-tech American wall ovens, but it serves my purposes just fine. I don't do fancy frosting on my cupcakes and all that useless, time-wasting ornamental junk. I bake to feed people."

Rose looked round the room. Lining one wall were giant sacks of ground corn, and lining another were shelf after shelf of blue mason jars, all labelled in Spanish. Rose burned to know what was in each jar and how to use it.

Balthazar stepped into the room. "For ten years I've been inventing new recipes using ground cornmeal. The golden porridge you were thumbing your nose at out there, Marj," he said, pointing to Rose, "happens to be called Polenta of Plenitude. And it's very useful. Unlike your American cupcakes. All style and no substance, I think."

As Balthazar launched into an oration on the various incarnations of ground corn, Sage and Leigh wandered off to investigate a rack of cooling strawberry pies, while Ty stepped back on to the patio to seek *amigas*. Purdy and Albert asked smart questions and settled into chairs to listen.

And so did Rose. After a while she noticed that some of the lines on her great-great-great-grandfather's face had softened into something that approximated a smile, or at least a non-frown.

"See, the Polenta of Plenitude gets made," Balthazar explained, "by stirring ground cornmeal in water and milk over an open flame." He poured a cup full of golden corn dust into a pot with two cups of milk, then swirled the pot over the iron bars of the stovetop grid. "Then you add honey, a sprig of rosemary, and this." Balthazar stepped over to the wall of blue jars and removed one labelled EL SAPO INFLADO.

Rose peered inside and saw a huge bullfrog leaning back against the side of the jar, his legs splayed out and both webbed forehands cradling his monstrous, swollen belly.

"The burp of a bloated bullfrog," he said, lowering the unscrewed jar to the boiling pot. The frog punched his gut with a tiny amphibian fist, then let out a rumbling, rolling belch that smelled, not surprisingly, like garlic.

A bubble grew out of the cornmeal, filling the entire pot, then swelling until it reached the ceiling of the tin shed before bursting in a sigh and dropping back into the pot.

"*There*," Balthazar huffed, stuffing the poor bloated bullfrog back on the shelf.

Balthazar dipped a spoon into the pot and handed it to Rose. The Polenta of Plenitude was some of the best stuff she'd ever tried: velvety, fresh, moist – the perfect balance of savoury and sweet.

"Mum and Dad!" Rose said. "You have to try this!"

Each tasted a spoonful of the masterful corn mixture.

"Wow!" said Purdy. "You've really made something special here, Balthazar!"

Balthazar swatted Purdy's compliment away like a fly, grumbling inaudibly. "I don't eat sweets any more," he said. "You eat too many sweets, you get too big to run away when people come after you. When this *masa* works its magic, you can't eat like most people do, stuffing themselves to the point where they're bloated like a couch potato. Eat a little of this *masa* as an appetiser, and you'll eat just enough of your main course to stay healthy. Unlike my *cat* over there, if you could call him that."

"What else would they call me?" came a low voice from a dark corner of the room.

Rose couldn't believe her eyes: a pudgy grey cat as wide around as a bowling ball lumbered out from behind a box and climbed up a ramp on to a rolling wooden chopping block. He sat upright on his haunches and licked under his front leg, which was quite thin compared to his thick face and rotund body. Most striking of all were his ears, which didn't stand straight up like a regular cat's but were pinched and rumpled into two folded lumps atop his wide face. "Balthazar, you should have told me we were having people over. I would have bathed. I'm in a shambles!"

"Whoa!" Sage exclaimed. "You have a talking cat?"

"*Unfortunately*," Balthazar replied. "He wandered into my parents' kitchen when I was fifteen, and he got his grubby claws on a batch of Chattering Cheddar Biscuits I made. He hasn't shut up since."

"Allow me to properly introduce myself since the old man can't bring himself to do it for me," the cat said. He sounded like a butler in a mansion outside of London. "My name is Asparagus the Green, but you should call me Gus."

"But you're *not* green," Sage said. "You're more of a dark grey."

"Minor details." The cat blinked. "I am a Scottish Fold, and—"

"Is that some kind of soldier or something?" asked Sage.

"It is the name of my breed. I am pure Scottish Fold, hence my exquisitely folded ears. I am not from Scotland, however. My dearly departed mother and father hailed from London. And who might you be?"

"This is my great-great-granddaughter Purdy Bliss; her husband, Albert; and her herbaceous children, Parsley, Sage, Marjoram, and Thyme."

"Rosemary," whispered Rose.

"Sure," Balthazar continued. "And they are here because—" Balthazar stopped and turned to Purdy. "Why *are* you here?"

"We're here for the translation of the Booke," she replied nervously. "We need it, now."

"Why?" he asked. "Can't you just use your own?"

"Our copy is indisposed at the moment."

"What do you mean, 'indisposed'?"

Rose and the rest of the family gathered around one of Balthazar's picnic tables, and Purdy recounted the tale of Aunt Lily. "So you see," Purdy concluded, "we need a copy of the Booke if we're to win."

Balthazar had listened to the story with his arms folded over his cardigan, his face growing steadily redder and redder. As Purdy concluded, his bushy black eyebrows sloped furiously downward to where they met in the centre of his furrowed brow. He stood up, scowled, then disappeared into his kitchen hut.

He reappeared a moment later carrying a dusty tome at least a foot thick, bound in ancient, disintegrating leather. He laid the book gingerly on the table and blew softly on the cover. A puff of black dust flew in Leigh's face.

"Is it customary in the land of Mexico to blow clumps of dust into the faces of small children?" Leigh coughed.

Gus bolted upright and dropped the shell of the cream puff he'd been licking back into his metal bowl. "I'm sorry; did the toddler just speak like a grown lady?"

"Of course I did!" Leigh answered indignantly. "This, from the talking cat!"

Rose peered at the book, which was thicker than her head. There were symbols printed on the cover, none of which she recognised.

"What does it mean?" she asked.

"It means 'Bliss Cookery Booke' in Sassanian," the old man said. "Sassanian's a dead language that was spoken by a tribe of ancient shamans in the Fertile Crescent. They made their medicines of wheat and honey and other sweet ingredients – those were the first magical bakers."

Balthazar pulled a short stack of parchment from the back of the Booke and slapped it down on the table. *Recipes.* They were written in English in perfect calligraphy, not a stroke out of place. "These," he said, "are the translations I've done so far. Nine in all."

"You've only translated nine recipes?" Albert asked, scratching at his beard and fanning out his armpits.

"Do you know how hard Sassanian is to decipher? I'm not about to do a rush job on something so important!"

"He's a bit. . . fastidious," Gus added.

"This, from a *cat*," Balthazar countered.

"We need access to as many recipes as is humanly possible by the time the Gala begins," said Purdy.

"And when's that?" said Albert.

"Day after tomorrow," said Purdy, pushing her sweaty bangs off her forehead. "We fly to Paris in just a few hours. Looks like we're toast."

Rose's heart plummeted. It was over before it ever began. There was no way she'd be able to defeat Lily – not when Lily had the Cookery Booke, not when Rose had nothing but her skills as a baker. It might have been different if she were able to read Sassanian, but now. . .

Balthazar stared off into the sky for a moment, snarling one side of his lip.

"You're just going to have to bring me along then," he announced, coughing. "I'll go pack my bags."

Chapter 3

ENTER THE MASTER OF CEREMONIES

ROSE SQUIRMED IN her seat aboard the 747 flying her and her family to Paris. The cabin lighting had been dimmed, and the muted roar of the jet engines was soothing; but Rose was having trouble falling asleep.

Her great-great-great-grandfather Balthazar was across the aisle from her, snoring. For the last hour, she'd watched a single droplet of spittle dangle from the corner of his mouth, then tuck itself up again, back and forth like a yo-yo, shivering with each massive snore, while Gus the cat, strapped into a baby sling against Balthazar's heaving, snoring chest, looked out in fury.

On the other side of Balthazar, Ty fiddled with a video game. Sage had pulled his legs on to the seat and fallen asleep Indian style, his hands on his knees.

"Excuse me, sir," said a voice from behind her. Rose

craned her neck around the seat to check on her baby sister, who'd grabbed the sleeve of a passing flight attendant. "I am very sorry to bother you. This juice box is a little saccharine and, frankly, unappealing."

The flight attendant gaped at the child, speechless.

From the next seat, Albert clapped a hand over Leigh's mouth. "She's fine with the juice box. Thank you."

Rose flopped back into her seat, a hot ball of anxiety churning in her stomach like a hurricane. She'd never felt so awful.

Purdy was sitting beside her. She reached over and took Rose's hand in hers. "I can practically hear your mind racing, Rosie."

Rose buried her head into the crook of her mother's arm. "I don't know if I can do this, Mama," she said. "What if I get the measurements wrong? What if I can't beat the egg whites fast enough? What if I sweat into the cupcakes, or just crumble and start crying, right there on TV?"

Purdy laughed. "Listen. You're a master already. You wanted more responsibilities in the kitchen; you got 'em. You've been an incredible sous-chef for the past nine months, even though the baked goods haven't been as magical as we'd like them to be. Now it's time for me to be *your* sous-chef; I'll be right there beside you every minute. And remember, I competed at the Gala when I was fifteen and came in third, with no sous-chef! So just imagine how well we'll do *together!*"

And it was then that the shaking in Rose's hands and the gurgling in her stomach finally abated, and her racing thoughts slowed to a jog, then a stroll, then sat down in the middle of her head and went to sleep.

Rose jolted awake as the jet touched down and bumped along the runway. Wiping sleep from her eyes, she leaned over her mother and looked out the window. Before this, Rose's whole world had been no bigger than Calamity Falls, with the occasional trip to her Aunt Gert Hogswaddle's house in the neighbouring county of Humbleton. Now it had burst at the seams and expanded to include the entire Atlantic Ocean.

The Bliss family got off the plane and picked up their luggage. Rose ogled all the signs written in French and listened to the French announcements piped in over the loudspeaker, none of which she understood. It was a new feeling, being a foreigner.

Riding in his baby sling on Balthazar's chest, Gus the Scottish Fold looked vaguely bored. Ty, on the other hand, swaggered through the long hall of the airport like he was having the time of his life. *"Hola,"* he said over and over again, in a near-whisper, to every long-legged woman they passed.

"We're in France, Ty," Rose reminded her brother. "Not Spain."

"Maybe some of these ladies are here on vacation from Spain," he retorted.

Sage was trying to imitate Ty's confident swagger. *"¡Hola!"* he called to a girl in a pink dress, and received a glare in response.

At the end of the long corridor was a man in a black suit and white gloves. He was holding up a poster board with BLISS printed on it in block letters.

Albert shook his hand. "Hi, hi," he said nervously, scratching the back of his head. "We're the Blisses. Last time we checked!"

"Oui," said the driver, the French word for *yes*, Rose knew.

The driver eyed Balthazar and Al cautiously. "Welcome to Paris," he said. "I am Stefan. Your car is right this way."

"To the Hôtel de Notre Dame, then?" Albert asked, fiddling with a few stapled papers on which he had printed their itinerary.

"No, no!" yelled Stefan. "The hotel will have to wait. You are late for the Gala orientation meeting with Jean-Pierre Jeanpierre, which means you are already treading on thin ice."

They had only just arrived, and already Rose was in trouble.

Rose's jaw dropped as Stefan stopped the car in front of the expo centre. It was a massive glass building with enormous banners on each side of the entrance. The banners were covered with pictures of giant cream puffs, tarts, and slices of gooey red velvet cake, with the words GALA DES GÂTEAUX GRANDS: 18–23 AVRIL printed in white letters.

Rose gulped. She knew the Gala des Gâteaux Grands was a big deal, but she wasn't expecting banners the size of blimps.

Stefan held the back door open while Rose and Purdy and the rest of the family piled out of the car. As they pushed through the giant revolving glass door in the front of the centre, a nervous woman with short golden hair and extremely thin lips, which she'd painted fire-engine red, ran over.

"Rosemary Bliss?" she said, taking Purdy's arm and

pulling her towards a set of giant double doors. "You are late for the orientation! You must hurry!"

"No, no, I'm *Purdy* Bliss," said Rose's mother.

The woman stopped in her tracks and eyed the rest of the group suspiciously. "Then which one of you is Rosemary Bliss? Who is our chef?"

Rose hooked her thumb against the chest of her hooded sweatshirt. "Me?"

Confusion flashed across the red-lipped woman's face. "Ah. I see. My name is Flaurabelle. I am chief assistant to Chef Jean-Pierre Jeanpierre. And you are late!" She ushered Rose through the double doors, with the rest of the Blisses following behind.

The room on the other side of the doors was immense. High ceilings arched overhead, with intricate hanging chandeliers. The floor was crowded with people sitting around large round tables. In the centre of each table was a giant crystal mixing bowl containing multi-coloured batter. All of the tables were filled except one.

Everyone turned to watch as the red-lipped woman led the Blisses to the empty table. Rose sat with Purdy and Ty on either side of her. "The batter is for decoration only," the red-lipped woman warned in a whisper. "We already had an incident this morning. Please do not eat the batter."

"OK," Rose said quietly. She turned to the people glaring at them from a nearby table. "Sorry we're late," she said.

"Americans," she heard someone sneer.

Just then the chandeliers went dark and a spotlight shone on a balcony on the back wall of the room. Pre-recorded orchestral music swelled as a man wearing a chef's coat made entirely of red velvet appeared atop the balcony. The man was clearly old – not as old as Balthazar, but far older than Purdy and Albert – and completely hairless. His head was bald, his cheeks and chin were bald – he even lacked eyebrows. His bald head was small compared to his rotund belly, giving him the overall appearance of a turtle.

How do I get myself into these things? Rose wondered.

"Ladies and gentlemen," boomed an announcer, "please welcome the inventor of chocolate éclairs, the pre-eminent pastry chef of France, and most importantly, the founder of the Gala des Gâteaux Grands, Chef Jean-Pierre Jeanpierre!"

As the audience applauded, Jean-Pierre Jeanpierre reached up, took hold of a set of handlebars hanging above the balcony, and stepped over the railing. The spotlight followed him as he soared down a zip line from the balcony to a stage on the other side of the room.

Chef Jeanpierre landed on the stage in a rumpled pile of red velvet. He huffed and puffed his way to a standing position and approached a podium, his arms held up like he was the pope.

Rose's stomach fluttered. She had read about Jean-Pierre Jeanpierre, of course. In a sense, he truly was the pope of baking. From her reading she knew that he took seven lumps of sugar in his morning coffee, that he'd had his hometown of St Aubergine renamed St Jeanpierre, and that he slept exclusively on pillows made of angel food cake, which he baked fresh every evening.

Whenever Rose thought that she'd become too obsessed with baking, she reminded herself about Jean-Pierre Jeanpierre.

Jean-Pierre's eyes glimmered wide from behind his spectacles. He tapped the microphone, then said, *"Bienvenue à la Gala des Gâteaux Grands."*

The room erupted into violent applause as everyone jumped to their feet and cheered.

"Please!" yelled Jean-Pierre. "Sit! Twenty of the world's fiercest culinary competitors – and their assistants – are in this room," said Jean-Pierre. "None of them as fierce as myself, of course, but this is why I exclude myself from competition."

As Jean-Pierre was boasting, Rose glanced round the room. At one table sat a slight, bespectacled man with his arms folded, holding whisks like knives. In front of his plate was a name tag that read WEI WEN, CHINA.

At another table, a young man smirked behind a name tag labelled ROHIT MANSUKHANI, INDIA. At still another table sat a lithe blond man who looked to be eight feet tall: Dag Ferskjold, Norway. He peered at the ceiling with a thousand-yard stare. None of the other contestants looked particularly happy or excited.

"Each morning at 9am," Jean-Pierre went on, "I will announce the surprise theme of the day. Past themes have included things like FLAKY. FLOURLESS. ROLLED. GREEN. Whatever crosses my mind as I wake. Where do the themes come from? Who knows!"

Rose turned round in her seat and glanced at the other side of the room. There was a tawny woman with short blonde hair gelled into spikes – Irina Klechevsky,

Russia – and a tall bald man with exceedingly white teeth – Malik Hall, Senegal. There was a short man with sallow skin and big lips – Victor Cabeza, Mexico – and a handsome man with shoulder-length brown hair – Peter Gianopolous, Greece. There was Fritz Knapschildt from Germany, King Phokong from Thailand, Niccolo Puzzio from Italy, and many more, all grown-ups wearing stern, competitive looks. They were out for blood.

What am I doing here? thought Rose.

Rose was relieved to spot a table with two French girls who looked like they could be in high school. Their name tags read MIRIAM DESJARDINS, FRANCE and MURIEL DESJARDINS, FRANCE; and, upon closer examination, it seemed that they were identical twins, though one had long, brown hair and the other one had short, brown hair.

Ty had seen them, too. He was leaning as far back in his chair as he could, raising and lowering his eyebrows at them. The girls were too busy staring at Jean-Pierre to notice.

"After I announce the theme," Jean-Pierre continued, "you will have one hour to collect a special ingredient of your own choosing. The rest of your ingredients must come from the Gala kitchen."

It suddenly occurred to Rose that Aunt Lily was probably sitting somewhere in that room at that very moment. Rose looked around and finally spotted the producers of *30-Minute Magic*, Ryan and Kyle, sitting at the table on the other side of the room. Both producers were typing on their phones; Lily herself was nowhere to be found.

Jean-Pierre paused for a minute to take a sip of tea. "At 10am, after you've collected your special ingredient, the competition will take place. There will be cameras filming you from every angle, capturing every turn of the spoon, every bead of sweat, every tear. You must love the cameras, and also ignore them."

Rose prayed that she wouldn't produce any tears for them to capture.

"After the baking you will face the judge's table, where your desserts will be sampled by the judge, who is myself. After that, I will announce who will move on to the next day of competition and who will be sent back to their houses to cry and relive the painful memories of what they did wrong, over and over, for the rest of their lives."

The audience tittered meanly.

"There will be five days of competition, with the final

day being a face-off between the top two competitors." Jean-Pierre paused to wipe his bare brow. "As always, competitors must work from memory. Anyone caught with a cookbook as they bake will be immediately tossed to the curb."

The *from memory* part was what worried Rose the most. The recipes in the Bliss Cookery Booke relied on precision – any deviation could alter not only the taste and texture of whatever she was trying to bake, but its magical properties as well. She and her mother would have to memorise the magical recipes perfectly in the hour before the baking commenced – that is, if Balthazar could manage to translate them.

"And, as always, no one who has previously participated in the Gala des Gâteaux Grands may participate again. If your assistant has previously baked in this competition, you must find a new assistant!"

Rose stared at her mother. Her mother stared back. *Don't panic,* she thought, trying to catch her breath. *Grandpa Balthazar is a professional. He can be my assistant.*

Balthazar was scratching Gus's pinched, rumpled ears. Rose leaned over and whispered, "You can be my assistant, right, Grandpa Balthazar?"

Balthazar shook his head. "Nope. I competed in the

first Gala des Gâteaux Grands in the nineteen fifties, when I was sixty-six. Lost flat-out. It was gruelling."

Rose looked at her father. "I know you never competed, Dad," said Rose.

Albert reached into the pocket of his trousers and pulled out a brown paper bag, then held it to his mouth and began to hyperventilate. "Rose," he managed in between puffs, "I can't be in front of cameras. Or audiences. I'm too shy. I'll get seasick. You'll be better off with Ty. You two were a good team when your mum and I went off to Humbleton, right?"

"Thyme, my sweet," said Purdy, "you'll help Rosie, right?"

Ty perked up, staring joyfully at the table where Miriam and Muriel Desjardins sat. "Sure! I'll get to be on TV, right?" Purdy nodded. "Anything for my beloved *hermana*." Ty practically shouted when he said *hermana*, hoping the French girls would hear him.

They didn't – but Jean-Pierre did.

"Shush your mouths!" he yelled. "You'll have the rest of the day to sort out your pairings. I will see you all tomorrow morning at 9am for day one of the competition."

With that, Jean-Pierre grabbed the handlebars, which

hoisted him higher and higher until he disappeared through a hole in the ceiling.

Rose looked again at her brother Ty, who gave her a double thumbs-up sign.

We are going to lose, she thought.

Chapter 4

SWEET, SWEET NOTHINGS

THE NEXT DAY, Rose examined her little Gala kitchen in the expo centre. It was one of twenty that were connected by an aisle of black and white checkered tiles that led to a raised platform at the front of the room with a microphone and a long oak dining table.

Hanging above the row of kitchens were balconies draped in red velvet, like special box seats at an opera. In the balcony above her, Rose saw Balthazar and Gus sitting with her parents and Sage and Leigh.

Across the black-and-white-tiled aisle stood Lily's kitchen. Lily was standing coolly behind a wooden chopping block, wearing, as usual, a black cocktail dress. She turned and winked at Rose as she tested the dials on her oven.

Rose sighed heavily, and Ty poked her in the shoulder. "What's bugging you, *mi hermana?*"

"This whole thing, it's too much pressure," she said.

Ty tousled her stringy black hair. "Don't worry, Rose. You're the best there is. And you've got me right here, all the way."

Ty had been so nice to Rose in the previous nine months that she almost couldn't believe it. But nice wasn't going to help her get the Booke back. She needed expert assistance. Still, it was comforting to have her older brother beside her.

"Thanks, Ty," she said.

Rose peered round her kitchen once more. On one side of the oven was a red refrigerator, and on the other was a wooden bookcase that served as a pantry. There were clear mason jars of flour, white sugar, brown sugar, baking powder, and cocoa powder, plus a brightly coloured cardboard box hidden in the back.

"What's this?" Ty asked Rose, picking up the box.

Rose took the box from Ty and recognised it immediately as a box of Lily's Magic Ingredient. "No!" said Rose. "What's this doing here?"

Rose marched across the aisle of black and white tiles

and stopped short in front of Lily's wooden chopping block.

"Why is this in my kitchen?" she demanded.

"It's in everyone's kitchen!" Lily replied, brushing a strand of black hair from her cheek. "I donated it, so it's part of everyone's allowable pantry items. Anyone can add a dash of Lily's Magic Ingredient – I think it'll really improve their results."

"It'll improve *your* results, you mean!" Rose cried. "Anyone who eats this stuff waxes poetic about you! The judge will just start talking about how amazing you are!"

"Can I help it if it has that particular side effect?" Lily winked.

The expo centre suddenly went dark, and Rose hurried back to her own kitchen. A set of roving purple spotlights focused on the centre of the ceiling, where a giant cupcake with a hollow centre hovered like a hot-air balloon.

"Ladies and gentlemen," boomed an announcer, "please welcome the inventor of crêpes suzette, the champion pastry chef of France, and the founder of the Gala des Gâteaux Grands: Chef Jean-Pierre Jeanpierre!"

Orchestra music soared as the giant cupcake sank slowly to the ground. Jean-Pierre Jeanpierre stepped out of it, dressed in his coat of red velvet, his hands clasped atop his wide belly. His beady eyes peered from behind his glasses as he stared out over the crowd.

He raised a microphone to his lips and said, "Remember, after I announce the theme, you'll have precisely one hour to plan and to gather your one special ingredient, one that is not found in the pantry."

"So now Lily can combine her Magic Ingredient with any of the magical recipes in the Booke, which will make it infinitely more powerful!" whispered Rose. "Can you believe this, Ty?"

But Ty was too busy staring across the black-and-white-tiled aisle. Miriam and Muriel Desjardins were looking casually at Ty. Ty was pretending not to notice, staring into the distance with his eyes wide and his mouth pursed, as if he were writing the lyrics to a painful love song in his head.

The twins had perfect faces, with sparkling eyes and pouting lips, chic haircuts, and expensive-looking clothes. They looked a year or two older than Ty, and an inch or two taller. They were definitely out of his league, but he would be the last one to admit it.

"And now. . . ," Jean-Pierre said over the thunder of a drumroll, "the theme of the day is. . . SWEET! You may interpret the theme however you wish. The cooking will commence in one hour. Go. Now!"

The lights snapped back to full in the room and the spectators in the opera boxes clapped as all of the bakers and their assistants began to confer in heated whispers.

SWEET. Rose could bake a hundred versions of the common cupcake, but today she was competing not only against the best bakers in the world, but also against her Aunt Lily, who could make any magical recipe in the Cookery Booke, plus add a dash of Lily's Magic Ingredient. To make it through this first round, she would need something from the Bliss Cookery Booke, and for that she needed Purdy and Balthazar.

As she waited for her mother and great-great-great-grandfather to join her on the expo floor, Rose glanced over at Lily. Lily was conferring with an impossibly small man wearing a calico jumpsuit of purple, white, and gold satin, the kind you'd find on a medieval clown. He was little, but he wasn't proportioned like a dwarf – it was as if he was a typically sized man who had been shrunken down. The top of his head barely reached Lily's hip. He had tanned skin, a bald head, thick black eyebrows, and a long, black moustache.

Lily's assistant? Rose wondered.

Balthazar and Purdy hurried up, with Albert, Sage, and Leigh trailing behind.

"Look at this," said Rose, holding up the box of Lily's Magic Ingredient. "She donated this to the Gala. Everyone's pantry is stocked with it."

"That wicked cheater!" Purdy yelled.

"I have just the thing to beat her," Balthazar said, handing her one of his perfectly handwritten sheets. "I translated this one a few months ago. It's aces."

With Ty looking over her shoulder, Rose read the recipe:

The Sweetest Cookie,
for the Relief of Human Sourness

It was in 1456, in the French city of Paris, that young Philippe Canard did confess to Sir Falstaffe Bliss that his sole wish on the occasion of his fifth birthday was that his notoriously sour, crabby, ill-tempered, and otherwise foul Grandmother might grant him a smile. Sir Bliss did feed these sweet cookies to the Countess Fifi Canard, who, at the

occasion of Philippe's birthday party, did hoist Philippe into
her arms, kiss his cheek, and smile so sweetly that young
Philippe himself did smile for the remainder of his life.

Sir Bliss did place four fists of WHITE FLOUR in the centre
of the wooden bowl. Into the flour he cracked one of the
CHICKEN'S EGGS, then poured an acorn of VANILLA and
one staff of melted COW'S BUTTER. Afterward, he did add
the LOVER'S SWEET WHISPERS, congealed in almond
butter.

"So that's our one special ingredient," Ty said. "'Lovers'
sweet whispers in almond butter.' That should be easy
enough to get. I'll just whisper into a jar."

Balthazar rolled his eyes. "No, kid. You'll need the
sweet whispers of *two* people who *are* in love, not *one*
person who *wishes* he was in love."

"Burn, *Abuelo*," Ty replied. "Burn."

There were a few more instructions, and then the
recipe ended with:

He did rest the cake in the oven HOT as SEVEN FLAMES
for the TIME of SIX SONGS and then fed the cookies to
the sour Countess, who remained sweet thereafter.

Just then Lily walked up, arm in arm with Jean-Pierre Jeanpierre. The short man she'd been talking with earlier was nowhere to be seen.

"Look!" Lily said, pointing at the scrap of paper with the recipe. "They're cheating!"

Purdy stepped between Lily and the recipe. "Lily, if you sunk any lower, they'd have to dredge you up from the bottom of the Seine."

Lily smiled at Jean-Pierre. "I really hate to have to tattle on children," she said. "I'm just trying to protect the integrity of the Gala."

Albert stepped in with a toothy grin. "No rule violations here, sir! The rules prohibit using a cookbook *while baking*. The kids have merely planned out their recipe. The paper will be gone come competition time."

Gus, still in the baby sling on Balthazar's chest, swatted Rose's ear till she leaned close, his whiskers tickling her cheek. "If I were you, I'd go now and get those sweet whispers. An hour goes by faster than you think."

"But where are we going to get lovers' sweet whispers?" Rose asked.

Gus squinted a minute, thinking. "In my first marriage, my dear Hilarie and I often exchanged sweet nothings while catching mice along the River Thames in London."

Gus was right – lovers did tend to congregate by water. The expo centre was only a few blocks from the Seine, the winding, snaky river that cut through Paris.

Rose reached up and scratched the soft grey fur under Gus's chin.

If it's possible for a cat to look bashful, at that moment, Gus did. "Thank you," he said. "Now go."

Though the riverbank was just a few minutes' walk from the Hôtel de Ville expo centre, Sage complained the entire time.

"Why am I even here? You and Ty are gonna do all the baking, and I'm just supposed to watch?" he whined. "With all those cameras around? *I* should be in front of the cameras! I could launch my stand-up comedy career. But no, you two get to do everything important, as usual."

Rose glanced over at Ty, then looked guiltily at the blue mason jar she was carrying, which she'd slathered on the inside with pale yellow almond butter. It was true. Sage rarely got the opportunity to do anything important. Of course, when he did, he usually made a mess of it.

"Why don't you be in charge of collecting the sweet

whispers?" said Rose. "In fact, you could collect *all* the special ingredients! We'll do the baking, you'll do the collecting, and then when we win, we'll introduce you on camera and you can launch your stand-up comedy career."

Ty looked at her like she was crazy, but Sage smiled and immediately stopped complaining. He took the blue mason jar from Rose and cradled it in his arms like it was an infant.

The morning light rippled across the Seine like a spilled canister of silver glitter. Rose thought that this may have been the most romantic place she'd ever seen, even more romantic than the overlook point on Sparrow Hill in Calamity Falls. She imagined building a hut on the stone riverbank and living there with Devin Stetson, baking croissants for passersby while he played guitar and collected change in a hat.

As she was plotting where on the river wall she'd build her hut, Rose spotted a man and a woman walking hand in hand. The man and the woman were staring at each other so lovingly and intently that the man tripped over a raised brick in the pavement and fell to his knees. The woman giggled as she hoisted him up again and kissed his cheek.

"Jackpot," Rose said.

Sage nodded and scooted ahead, falling into step a few feet behind the couple. He opened the blue jar and held it up to the back of their heads, trailing behind as close as he could without running into them.

It worked for a few seconds, until Sage sneezed and the man whipped around. "What are you doing, kid?" he said.

Sage snapped the jar closed so as not to catch any less-than-sweet whispers in the almond butter. "Uhhh. . ."

Ty jogged over to Sage. "You'll have to excuse my brother," Ty said. "He's collecting fireflies."

"But it's the *daytime*," said the woman.

Ty covered Sage's ears with his hands. "He *thinks* he's collecting fireflies," he whispered. "Poor kid hallucinates fireflies wherever he goes. Carries this jar everywhere and just keeps swiping it through the air. We don't have the heart to tell him the truth."

The man and woman nodded sympathetically as Ty removed his hands from Sage's ears. "You keep chasing those fireflies, son!" the man said, rustling Sage's curly red hair. The pair waved and headed off towards the Eiffel Tower.

"I heard that," groaned Sage. "Thanks a lot for turning me into a crazy person."

Rose and her brothers sat down at an outdoor café overlooking the river. A waiter in a starched white shirt, black trousers, and a white apron handed them menus.

"*Merci,*" Rose said, blushing. She knew how to say a few words in French, but she had a hard time pulling off the accent.

"*De rien,*" replied the waiter.

Two tables over, Rose spotted a handsome gentleman with a jaunty wave of grey hair sitting with an elegant woman in a silky red dress. Something on the woman's hand was glinting in the sun. It was so bright that at first Rose thought it must be the face of a watch, but it wasn't on the woman's wrist; it was on her finger. Rose realised it could only be a diamond ring, the biggest she had ever seen.

"Look at those two!" Rose said.

The woman leaned over the table and put a finger underneath the man's chin.

"*Je te quitte,*" said the woman.

"*Ne me quitte pas!*" answered the man.

Sage nodded, then snaked along the ground towards

the table where the couple was whispering their sweet nothings.

"Wow," said Ty, admiring the couple. "Look at that. Maybe I should give up Spanish and learn French instead."

Sage slunk to the base of the table and held up the mason jar.

"*Je te quitte*," the woman repeated.

"*Ne me quitte pas!*" the man answered back.

As Rose watched, the almond butter inside the jar slowly turned grey. It was odd. Rose always thought love would be red.

Sage slammed the jar closed and popped up from the ground, banging his head on the bottom of the couple's table. The tiny cup of espresso that the man had been drinking hurtled skyward, bathing the man's elegant grey hair in steaming brown coffee.

"*Ahhh!!!*" he screamed. "*Qu'est-ce qui ce passe!*"

Sage scrambled from beneath the table as the waiter headed straight for him, a basket of bread in his hands. He pelted Sage in the face with a roll and cried, "Don't come back here, you strange children!"

Rose and Ty jumped out of their seats and took off for the Hôtel de Ville expo centre. Sage, with sweat on his brow, a bump on his head, and crumbs in his face, raced past them, then turned around victoriously, holding the blue mason jar high above his head. "Got it!"

When Rose and her brothers returned to their kitchen in the expo centre, Jean-Pierre had just finished his investigation about their supposed cheating. "Because the cooking had not officially begun," he said to Lily and the Blisses, "there has been no infraction of the rules."

"Oh, good!" Lily said. "I would hate to see these kids kicked out of the competition." She looked at Rose and gave her an icy smile as she returned to her kitchen.

Rose closed her eyes and focused on recalling the recipe. Balthazar's calligraphy was so unique – so ornate, so perfect – that Rose found she could easily picture the recipe as he had written it, including the ingredients, the measurements, the temperatures, and the times.

She 'read' the ingredients out loud to herself. "White flour, eggs, vanilla, butter, lovers' whispers."

Purdy wrapped her arms around Rose and squeezed. "Go get 'em, lovie."

Rose looked down at her little sister. "Wish me luck, Leigh."

Leigh ignored Rose. "The décor in here is dreadful," she said, looking at the ceiling and sighing. "If a space is meant to be grand, it must at least *attempt* to employ the conventions of rococo. Where are the whimsical stucco stylings of the Wessobrunner School? Lily Le Fay prefers the Wessobrunner School."

"What is she talking about?" Rose asked.

Purdy sighed. "Before we left home, I tried to whip up a batch of Scones of Simplification. Even though I knew they weren't perfect, I fed her one this morning and it backfired. And now she's fixated not only on Lily, but on art history as well."

Rose shook her head, wondering if she'd ever get her sweet little sister back.

Jean-Pierre waddled from his floating cupcake carriage to the front of the stage and seized the microphone. "The time has come. You will have one hour in which to prepare your first dessert. You may keep track of time there!" Jean-Pierre pointed to the wall above the doors, where there hung a big black clock in the shape of a baking timer. "Ready. Set. Bake!"

Purdy hurried off with Sage and Leigh to join Balthazar and Albert in the opera box, leaving Rose and Ty to swim – or sink – in cookie dough.

Rose hurried to her ingredients and found a sack of flour and a tiny brown bottle of vanilla. She opened the red refrigerator and pulled out a carton of eggs and a stick of butter. She arranged her ingredients on the wooden chopping block in front of a mixing bowl and exhaled noisily. "OK. Here goes. Ty, can you get the measuring spoons?" she said.

But Ty was already too busy talking to the camera. He leaned casually against the chopping block with his arms crossed over his chest, flexing his biceps. Rose recognised the pose, another standard weapon in Ty's arsenal of handsomeness – he called it 'The Manly Man.'

"There's nothing harder than baking," he crooned into the camera, running his fingers along the stiff red spikes on his forehead, "or more rewarding. I've sacrificed everything to be here. My spring break. . . everything. It makes dating difficult, of course, because I pretty much bake from the moment I wake up until the moment I take off my shirt at night and go to sleep. But I'd be willing to lay down my spatula for the right woman." He winked into the camera as it drifted over to Rose.

It was a curious sensation, being filmed. There was something about knowing you're being watched

– knowing that someone thinks you are interesting enough to record your face and actions and words for eternity – that was a little bit dizzying. It propelled Rose forward as she gathered the measuring cups and dumped two cups of flour into the bowl.

"Whoa," said Ty, pointing to Aunt Lily's kitchen, where no less than seven cameras were capturing her every elegant move. "Why don't we have that many cameras?"

"It's not about the cameras, Ty," Rose said. "Just get the blue mason jar."

Ty retrieved the jar, opened it, and used a metal spoon to scoop up every last bit of greyed almond butter. He plopped all of it into the bowl with the rest of the ingredients.

Rose stirred, and the batter turned blood red.

"Ah, red! The color of passion!" said Ty, winking again at the camera.

As Rose continued to stir, the red dissolved into a gritty black. She stirred and stirred, and the mixture grew thick and gummy and heavy, until finally it stuck together in a tight black ball in the bottom of the bowl.

"This isn't right!" Rose said. She glanced at the big timer on the wall – there were only thirty minutes left, just enough time to bake the cookies.

Rose looked up at her family in the balcony. Purdy smiled and gave Rose a thumbs-up, but Rose could tell that Purdy looked worried.

Rose gouged spoonfuls of the thick black mess on to a baking sheet, then tossed them into the oven. "Maybe they'll come out all right," she whispered. "Please let them come out all right."

When the timer reached zero, a deafening clang reverberated through the expo centre.

"Spoons down!" boomed Jean-Pierre Jeanpierre. "Marco will now bring your SWEET desserts to me at the judge's table, and I will sample each one."

A dashing, tawny man wearing a white-gloved uniform placed Rose's finished plate of blackened cookies on a rolling silver cart as long as a helicopter blade, along with the nineteen other contestants' plates. He practically flew up the black-and-white-tiled aisle towards the stage at the front, then laid the desserts in front of Jean-Pierre.

All of the twenty contestants filed up from their kitchens and formed a line facing the bottom of the stage.

"There are twenty of you right now," Jean-Pierre

intoned, "but in five minutes' time, there will be only ten. *Bonne chance.*"

Rose's cookies were first in line on the silver tray, although they looked more like shrivelled monkey heads than sugar cookies – nothing like what Sir Falstaffe Bliss must have presented to the sour Countess Fifi Canard.

Jean-Pierre took one of the gummy cookies and sank into it with his teeth. Rose swore she could hear a tooth cracking.

Jean-Pierre snapped his fingers, and Marco held a delicate silver bowl up to his lips. Jean-Pierre spat the bite he'd taken into the silver bowl, looked at Rose with dead eyes, and cleared his throat. Then he moved on to the next plate, saying nothing at all.

Down the line, Lily put a hand on either cheek and mouthed *Oh, no!* to Rose in a show of sympathy as false as her long black locks.

That's it. I ruined everything, Rose thought. *Now we'll never get the Cookery Booke back.*

Chapter 5

QUIET AS A MOUSE

JEAN-PIERRE STOOD ON the stage with Marco, the handsome waiter, and Flaurabelle, his red-lipped assistant, whispering back and forth.

Rose couldn't understand what she'd done wrong. Too much flour? Not enough vanilla? Had the lovers' whispers been tainted?

"I'm going to find Mum," she said, sulking off in the direction of the opera box at the side of the room.

"Wait up, *mi hermana!*" said Ty.

When they found the box, Rose fell into Purdy's arms. "Jean-Pierre spat my cookie into a bowl!" she sobbed.

"He sure did," Balthazar grumbled. "Are you sure you captured lovers' whispers?"

"Totally sure," said Sage. "The woman had a ring the size of a kiwi."

"But what did they *say*?"

Sage shrugged. "It was, like, '*Fi fi fah fah fah. Hoh huh hee huh huh.*' Pretty much exactly like that."

"No, no, dude," said Ty. "It was, like, '*Zha-tah keet. Na-mah keet-pah. Zha-tah keet. Na-mah keet-pah.*' Which I assumed meant, like, 'You are so hot' and 'I know I am so hot.' Right, *Abuelo*?"

Balthazar shook his head. "No! Wrong. '*Je te quitte*' means 'I'm leaving you,' and '*Ne me quitte pas*' means 'Don't leave me.' You trapped break-up whispers instead of lovers' whispers. That's what made the cookies taste bitter and look like – well, like they looked. Also, don't call me *Abuelo*. I was born in New Jersey."

Just then Jean-Pierre took up his microphone and cleared his throat. "I have now made my decision. Half of you will be moving on in the competition, and half of you will be swept away on a wave of shameful tears. The bakers who will be joining us tomorrow are, in no particular order. . ."

As Jean-Pierre rattled off name after name, shouts of joy wafted up from other kitchens. Rohit Mansukhani, the baker from India, did a victory dance. Wei Wen, the slight baker from China, nodded courteously. Dag Ferskjold, the tall Norwegian, pounded his fists on his cutting board and broke down in tears of relief. Miriam and Muriel, the French twins Desjardins, jumped up and down like schoolchildren.

Ty jumped with them.

"You're supposed to be rooting for *our* team, Ty," said Rose.

"I am!" he said. "But I'm also rooting for Miriam and Muriel."

Finally, Jean-Pierre paused and looked out over the crowd. "I have named the eight contestants who will be advancing in the competition. Other than the victor, only one name remains," he said.

Rose shook her head. She knew she was finished.

"Bliss."

Rose's eyes darted around the room. Was there another competitor named Bliss? Or had she, by some miracle, been allowed to continue on?

"Oh, thank goodness!" Purdy screamed, hoisting Rose up in the air.

"The rest of you," Jean-Pierre continued, "may pack up your spatulas and leave the premises." Irina Klechevsky from Russia threw her hands up in the air, while Malik Hall from Senegal dropped to his knees and cursed the sky. Victor Cabeza from Mexico hung his head, while Peter Gianopolous stormed out of the expo centre. Fritz Knapschildt and the others simply collected their utensils and walked off towards the door, sighing.

That could have been me, Rose thought.

Jean-Pierre cleared his throat. "Congratulations to the nine bakers, though I use the term loosely. Some of the so-called sweet desserts were an abominable, dismal mess. I have been forced to allow these people to pass through to day two only because half of our contestants didn't finish their baked goods in time. Those of you who've barely skated by – and you know who you are – will be shown no mercy tomorrow."

Rose pictured Jean-Pierre slicing her head off with a guillotine made out of sheet cake.

"Our winner for today," Jean-Pierre went on, "is a woman whose decadent chocolate creation managed to tickle even myself, the world's foremost expert on chocolate. The magnificent woman who has rescued the morning from insignificance is. . . Lily Le Fay!"

Rose peered into Jean-Pierre's eyes as he announced the winner. His blue eyes had darkened so that Rose couldn't tell where pupils ended and irises began, just as Leigh's eyes had darkened when she ate the entire

Pound-for-Pound Cake tainted with Lily's Magic Ingredient. Jean-Pierre hadn't eaten quite that much, and his body was considerably larger than Leigh's, so Rose hoped that the effects would be short-lived; but still, they were unmistakable. Lily could have made instant mashed potatoes with her Magic Ingredient and he would have proclaimed it the most genius thing he'd ever eaten.

I don't stand a chance against her magic, Rose thought.

Lily ran to the stage, where Jean-Pierre placed a silver tiara on her head. Dozens of cameras swarmed, bulbs flashed, and Lily smiled.

"How does it feel to win, Lily?" one of the cameramen asked.

"Oh, I'm humbled just to be here," she said.

That's when Rose spotted the tiny man in the harlequin costume. He cocked his bald head to the side and peered up into the crowd from beneath the bushy black caterpillars of his eyebrows. His eyes flashed green, and Rose could swear she saw him wink at her from all the way down on the stage.

"Ty," Rose said, pulling on his sleeve. "Do you see that? Who is that guy?"

"What guy?"

"The little guy standing next to Lily."

Ty peered down over the stage. "There's no little guy, *mi hermana*."

Rose checked again. Ty was right. There was no longer anyone standing next to Lily except reporters and cameramen.

Ty patted Rose on the head. "I think you need a nap."

When they got back to the family's suite at the Hôtel de Notre Dame, Rose locked herself in the room she was sharing with Leigh and couldn't be coaxed out, not even by the aroma of boxed macaroni and cheese being heated up in the suite's miniature kitchen.

"Rose!" Leigh called through the door. "Your level of despondence rivals that of Van Gogh. Are you going to cut your ear off over a few burned cookies? You're being selfish and maudlin. Besides, my blanky is inside and you've locked me out blanky-less! Open the door!"

"Rose, honey, open the door," said Purdy. "What happened today wasn't your fault. We just weren't prepared."

Rose let out a huge sigh.

"We'll be prepared for tomorrow," said Albert. "But you gotta come help us figure out what to do."

"I want to go home," Rose said. "There are just too

many ways everything can go wrong. It's not a fair match, me and her. She's using her Lily's Magic Ingredient stuff, and I just have our old family recipes."

"Check your maths on that one," Balthazar grunted. "Last I checked, Lily had a team of one. You have six people and a talking cat out here, all working for you."

"True," said Gus. "Although Lily has the Magic Ingredient on her side as well. And some very rare items in blue mason jars as well. The two in conjunction are lethal."

"What rare items?" asked Balthazar.

Rose listened closer, pressing her ear to the door.

"Today she used the whinny of a camel-horse," Gus replied.

Rose threw open the door. *"Really?* How do you know?"

Everyone was gathered in a circle around an ottoman, peering down at Gus, who was ignoring everyone, running his rough tongue over his silky grey paw.

"I was watching her as she worked," he said, sitting back on his hind legs. "More importantly, I was listening. When the batter was almost done, she opened a blue mason jar over the bowl, and I distinctly heard the neighing of a horse. You know." Gus did his best impression of a braying horse, complete with kicking the dirt with his hind legs.

"What's a camel-horse?" Ty asked.

Balthazar glared sideways at Ty like Ty had just asked how to spell his own name. "What do you teach these children? A camel-horse! Camel-horses were bred by a trader of chocolate in ancient Samarkand named Elmurod. Elmurod noticed that everyone who petted camel-horses instantly felt calm and peaceful, so he invented a chocolate confection that contained the magical whinny of the camel-horse. He called them Bless-Me Brownies, and, like petting the actual animal, they made people feel calm and peaceful – a feeling that's always been in short supply, if you ask me."

"Where did she ever get the whinny of a camel-horse?" Purdy asked. "There are only a few blue mason jars with the whinnies of camel-horses left in the world, and they should be sitting in a museum, not wasting away in Lily's brownies."

"She's *El Tiablo*," Ty whispered.

"What?" Balthazar croaked.

"*Nada.*"

"Well then, we'll just have to be better!" growled

Albert. "We should build our own arsenal of super-exotic ingredients, more exotic even than the ones we brought with us, and tailor our recipes to offset and override whatever Lily does."

"But how can we offset her recipe if we don't know what she's going to bake?" Rose asked.

"Duh. We need a spy," said Sage, leaning casually over the back of the couch. "And clearly, I am the most qualified."

"Based on what?" said Ty.

"Based on my powers of disguise." He pulled the collar of his T-shirt up to the bridge of his nose so that just his eyes and red Brillo hair were showing.

All of a sudden, Leigh shrieked and scrambled on to a chair. "Vermin!" she cried. She pointed towards the baseboard by the door, where Rose saw a tiny grey mouse, no bigger than a Ping-Pong ball, scampering towards the corner of the room.

"Nobody move," whispered Gus. "There will be absolute silence as I commence the hunt. Does anyone have a small rifle or crossbow?"

"Gus, you useless animal," said Balthazar. "Do it yourself!"

Gus swished his tail. "I don't want his disease-ridden coat

in my mouth! He probably has mumps, or rubella. These creatures aren't vaccinated, you know!"

"Gus," whispered Purdy, who had perched atop the couch. "Please."

"Fine," said Gus. He lumbered down from the ottoman and slunk across the floor to the corner of the room, where the little mouse was shivering.

"Would someone please ready a breath mint for me?" Gus said. "I'll need it when this is over."

Then Gus leaped forward and seized the mouse in his jaws. Instead of gulping down the furry little morsel, Gus waddled across the floor and hopped on to the kitchen counter, where he grabbed a drinking glass between his paws. He spat out the mouse and, before the dazed creature could run, flipped the glass down over it, trapping it underneath.

"That's noble of you, *gato*, to spare the mouse's life," said Ty.

"I'm not being kind, playboy. I am being practical. Mouse isn't tasty enough for my refined palate." Gus contemplated the furry creature languishing under the drinking glass. "Although I have an idea. If we need a spy, the mouse could do the job well enough. He's small, and if he perishes in the line of duty, no one will miss him."

"But a mouse can't *talk*," said Rose.

"Think outside the box, child," said Gus. "I can talk, can't I?"

Purdy turned to Balthazar, who was leaning back in a frilly brocade chair. "Could we make the mouse talk?"

Balthazar thought for a minute, pressing his back into the chair and clinging to the sides with his big, pockmarked hands. "Sure," he said. "But if this mouse is going to be half as chatty as the cat, I'm not sure I want to."

Everyone in her family seemed so optimistic about Rose winning the competition. Why couldn't she feel optimistic about herself?

Six flames and five songs later, the Chattering Cheddar Biscuits – made with the only cheese on hand, the mac and cheese powdered "cheese" – were puffed and crusty and tinged a curious, unnatural shade of orange. Balthazar slipped a hot biscuit under the glass to the little mouse. The mouse looked around nervously, then dived into the biscuit and devoured the whole thing.

Balthazar lifted the glass as the mouse sat back, bloated. He crinkled his pink, bulbous nose in an expression that looked suspiciously similar to disgust.

Suddenly the little mouse opened his mouth and spoke.

"You call that *cheese*?" he piped up in a thick French accent. His long front teeth got caught on his bottom lip as the words tumbled out. "Ah! I am talking! Why am I talking? Who are you people? Don't you know better than to give fake cheese to a mouse from France?"

Rose held out her hand to the mouse, and he stepped on it, one paw at a time. "I have very sharp teeth!" he said. "If you try to crush me, I will bite you!"

"I'm not going to crush you," Rose said gently. "You are a lucky mouse, Monsieur. . ."

"*Jacques*," answered the mouse. "*Je m'appelle Jacques*. Why am I lucky?"

"Well," answered Rose, "not only have you been given the power of speech, but you have also been hired as a spy."

"A spy?" Jacques marvelled. "But I couldn't possibly be a spy! I am a musician, a flautist! I was going home to practise when that demon snatched me up in his jaws!"

"What if we were to pay you?" Rose replied. "In cheese. *Real* cheese."

Chapter 6

THE SEVENTEENTH FLOOR

AND WHERE IS the room of this chef of the dark arts?"
Jacques asked after they'd explained everything and
gone out to buy Jacques's required form of payment:
a fine Roquefort cheese.

He was sitting on the knee of Rose's jeans as she
sat back on the couch. Albert, Purdy, and Balthazar sat
next to Rose; and Ty, Sage, and Leigh leaned over the
back of the couch and watched Jacques. Gus had slunk
off to the bathroom to clean his paws. At that point it
was four in the afternoon, after what had been a long
morning, and everyone was yawning quietly.

"We don't actually know," Rose admitted. "She's
famous. When famous people come to the Hôtel de
Notre Dame, where do they stay?"

Jacques shuddered. "The Fantasy Floor. It's an

armoured compound at the top of the building. The regular elevator doesn't go there; there's a hidden elevator. I know where it is, but it is too dangerous. I am sorry; I cannot do it."

Purdy went to the fridge, retrieved the hunk of Roquefort, and unwrapped it. She waved the white, creamy slab underneath Jacques's pointed little nose. Rose wrinkled her own nose; the stuff smelled like armpits and was dotted with black mould. Jacques, however, was overcome with desire.

"Ah!" he cried. "I cannot resist! I will risk my life for this cheese. I have sunk so low!"

With a scrabbling of tiny claws, Jacques vaulted off Rose's knee and disappeared into a hole in the wall.

The Blisses counted the minutes while their intrepid mouse spy was gone, fretfully pacing and saying very little. But three hours later Jacques scurried back into the centre of the living room.

He lifted his little nose at Rose. His eyes were wide, and he was shaking and drenched in sweat. "*Mademoiselle.* Please."

Rose bent down and laid her hand flat on the floor. Jacques climbed on to her palm, and Rose carefully lifted him to the kitchen counter. He sat back on his haunches and wiped the sweat from his fur as the family arranged themselves around him to hear his report.

"*Alors*, it was a harrowing journey," he said, "but after many great exertions, I at last found myself crouching between two cans of beans in an open cabinet in the witch's kitchen. The air was filled with the smell of—"

"Baking?" Sage asked.

"*Non!*" said Jacques. "*Evil.* While I waited, I was made fun of by a brutish cockroach. I ran him off. And then the witch came into the kitchen. She stood at the stove and looked through a thick book with a brown leather cover."

"The Cookery Booke!" Purdy gasped.

"It's here, in *this hotel?*" said Albert. "Storm the Fantastic Floor! Or whatever it's called."

"After a while the witch closed the book and left the kitchen. When she returned, she was pulling a large portable wardrobe."

"A wardrobe?" Albert asked incredulously.

"Yes," said Jacques. "A great wardrobe of dark wood. When she opened the double doors, I saw jars. Dozens of mason jars, tinted blue. I couldn't see what was in the jars. Out loud to herself the witch said, 'SOUR.' And then she took down one of the jars. Into a bowl she poured flour and a bunch of other things, and then she poured the jar over the bowl. When she did, there rose from the bowl the sound of crying. And then she put in a jar of capers."

"Capers?" said Ty, examining his cuticles. "Those little sour green things? In a cake?"

Purdy gave a quick nod. "She's making Sourpatch Pie," she said. "SOUR was one of the categories when I competed in ninety-two. She's probably running through the recipe just in case that's one of the categories. Did she do anything else?"

"*Oui*," answered Jacques. "From a cardboard box she put a dash of the powder into the pie."

Ty muttered, "Lily's Secret Ingredient."

"Then something happened that made my fur stand on end! From the bowl came a sinister whisper: *Lilllyyyyy. . .*"

"Did you see her do anything else?" Purdy asked.

"*Oui, madame*," he said. "Many, many things."

Jacques recounted the sound of a powerful Scandinavian soprano – clearly a Soprano Wedding Cake, according to Purdy. "Probably for the SUGARLESS category."

"Then there was purple smoke—"

"Could be a Jittering Jelly Roll," said Albert. "For the ROLLED category."

"There was a green explosion—"

"Springtime Soufflé. Definitely AIRY," Purdy noted.

And then Jacques described an eerie silence accompanied by an iridescent swirl and the howling of a low, empty wind.

"A Hold-Your-Tongue Tart," said Purdy. "Though I don't know what category she's intending that for. You know something about Hold-Your-Tongue Tarts, don't you, kids?"

Rose, Ty, Sage, and Leigh exchanged looks. Rose remembered, after Lily had visited them in Calamity Falls, the way her tongue had gone numb and limp whenever she tried to talk about Lily.

"Now that we know some of what she's preparing," said Purdy, pacing around the ottoman in circles, "we need to gather our own stock of extra-special ingredients so we'll have weapons to fight back with, no matter what the secret theme of the day happens to be."

Balthazar disappeared into his room and returned lugging a suitcase of blue linoleum that looked like it had been made before World War II. He raised the lid, and Rose gasped at the rows of miniature blue mason jars tucked neatly inside, each topped with a handwritten label.

"Like any good kitchen magician, I don't travel anywhere without a supply. I have some of what we might need here," he said, "but this is just a limited sampling. We'll need more."

"We'll need to think of all the possible surprise categories," said Purdy, "then pick recipes that can beat Lily's, even with the addition of her Magic Ingredient – recipes that are the most incredible, delicious recipes in the whole Booke, recipes she might not know about 'cause I doubt she's tried all six hundred and twenty-three. Then Balthazar will translate the recipes – quickly – Rose will memorise, and we'll have gathered the required ingredients ahead of time."

"Thank you, Jacques," said Purdy, looking to where Jacques had been sitting. "You've been very helpful. . ."

But Jacques was no longer there. "Where did he go?"

Gus shrugged his shoulders. "I warned him to leave and never come back."

"But why?" Rose cried. "He was so kind to us! He risked his life!"

"It is written in the *Book of the Scottish Fold*. When a Fold encounters a mouse, the Fold will warn the mouse never to return. If the mouse disobeys the warning, anything goes, as they say."

"We can debate the politics of cat-and-mouse relations later," said Purdy. "I do hope Jacques returns so we can thank him, but for now, we have to get to work."

The family sat around on the living room couches for the rest of the evening, sorting out how to survive the competition against their formidable, cheating, high-heeled opponent.

Purdy turned to a fresh sheet of paper from Rose's notebook. She wrote down the possible categories for the remaining days of the competition based on categories she'd competed in during her time at the Gala and stories from friends who had competed as well.

She wrote:

Puffed
Short
Filo
Cheesy
Chocolate

Airy
Sugarless
Flaky
Rolled
Sour

Rose sat next to Balthazar, who held his Sassanian version of the Cookery Booke open on the lap of his trousers. He described various recipes as he turned to them, and the family debated back and forth together about which would be the most exotic and special, until eventually they settled on a few good options.

"Better-Than-Anything Banana Bread will beat Lily's Soprano Wedding Cake in the SUGARLESS category any day," said Balthazar.

"And I bet an Angel's Breath Food Cake would beat a Springtime Soufflé in the AIRY category," said Purdy. "It's much airier."

Ty and Albert took turns writing out ideas on Rose's note paper while Balthazar looked through the ancient copy of the Booke, telling Rose and Purdy about each recipe. Sage and Gus shouted out their opinions while Leigh napped in a corner.

The final list looked like this:

Puffed – Nectar-of-Joy Cream Puffs

Filo – Born Yesterday Baklava

Cheesy – Sublime Danish

Chocolate – Disappearing Devil's Food Cake

Airy – Angel's Breath Food Cake

Sugarless – Better-Than-Anything Banana Bread

Flaky – Crazed Croissants

Rolled – Ravishing Rugelach

Sour – Double Orange Whoopie Pie

When they had finally finished with the list, it was midnight, and Purdy declared that everyone should get some sleep, particularly Rose and Ty, who had to bake early in the morning.

"But we won't be ready in the morning!" Rose protested. "Balthazar can't possibly translate all these recipes by then! And we can't have gathered all the necessary ingredients by then, either!"

"Calm down, Rosie, honey," said Albert. "It'll all work itself out. Balthazar can wake up early and start translating, and we'll still have an hour before baking tomorrow to gather the ingredients we need."

And so Rose reluctantly went to her room and lay down on her bed opposite a snoring Leigh.

She felt a little better having an idea of what categories might be coming up and what to do if they did, but she had no idea how she would get through tomorrow morning with no translated recipes and no ingredients.

She tried to fall asleep, but she kept hallucinating the sound of flute music. *I must be having some sort of bizarre nightmare,* she thought. The music seemed to be coming from the wall, from underneath a writing desk in the corner. After a moment, Rose hopped out of bed and followed the sound. She discovered a small hole in the baseboard through which she could hear the flute music more clearly.

"Hello?" she whispered into the hole.

The flute music stopped. After a moment Jacques poked his fuzzy nose through the hole.

"Jacques!" she whispered. "You're back!"

"I am not *back*," he replied. "I live in this hole, and I am doing my nightly practice. But I have not returned. I have not disobeyed the warning of the Scottish Fold. It is written in the *Book of Mouse* that I must stay away until the warning has been rescinded."

"There's a *Book of Mouse*, too?" asked Rose.

Jacques emerged from the hole, looking left and

right, then sat back on his haunches. He was carrying a miniature silver flute the size of a toothpick. "Every mouse has a copy of the *Book of Mouse*," he said. "It is a history of mice, their oppression by humans and cats, and their glorification by insects and small birds."

Rose nodded. "We had a book like that. It's a collection of our family's magical recipes, sort of a magical family history. Some of the recipes are good; some are dangerous. We never used the dangerous ones. Except once, by accident."

"You say you *had* the book? Where did it go?" Jacques asked.

"It's the one you just saw in that suite on the Fantasy Floor," said Rose. "That's the whole reason we're here. To beat my Aunt Lily in a baking contest and get that book back. But I don't think I can do it."

"Your mind is heavy," said Jacques, patting Rose's knee with his tiny paw, which was the size of a lentil. "Which is why you are awake at such a late hour."

"It's true," said Rose. "I just wish I could get the Booke back tonight. There's no way I can win against Lily. I'm not a good enough baker."

Rose pondered a minute, then trapped Jacques between her palms and ferried him into Sage and Ty's room, where her brothers had already fallen asleep.

"Guys! Ty! Sage! Wake up! I have an idea!" Rose shouted, drowning out the sound of Jacques's pleas. "Instead of waiting around to lose tomorrow morning, why don't we sneak up to the Fantasy Floor tonight and steal the Booke back once and for all!"

"What?" Sage said groggily.

"Rose, go back to bed," said Ty.

Rose ran to Ty's bed and shook him awake by the shoulder, holding Jacques captive in her other palm. "We can sneak up to Lily's room, steal the Booke back, and go home and fix Calamity Falls tomorrow. Wouldn't that be easier?"

Ty sat up in bed, his eyes still closed. "Yeah, I guess. . ."

"Sage, don't you want this whole thing over with?" said Rose.

"It's kind of unlike you to want to break into someone's room and steal something, Rose."

"I don't want to steal; I just want to make sure we get the Booke back, and I don't think I can do it by winning the contest," she replied.

Jacques shook his narrow little head. "*Non, non.* I cannot show you how to get up to the Fantasy Floor. It is too dangerous."

Rose thought for a moment. "I suppose a slice of Brie wouldn't change your mind?" she said.

Jacques sat in the front pocket of Rose's hooded sweatshirt as she and her brothers walked through the hotel lobby. On one side of the room stretched the hotel's ornate front desk. A flower arrangement dominated the room's centre, towering nearly to the massive chandelier hanging from the frescoed ceiling.

According to the huge clock above the front desk, it was half an hour past midnight. While the chandelier above them burned brightly, the rest of the lights in the room were dimmed, and the lobby was nearly empty.

Rose and her brothers continued past the elevators to the hotel café and a door marked TOILETTE. On the other side of the door was a red velvet staircase.

"Keep going," Jacques instructed.

They climbed the stairs and came to a hallway cordoned off by a delicate chain. A sign hanging from the chain read PRIVÉ.

"That means 'private,' doesn't it, Jacques?" said Rose. "We can't go in."

"You wanted to get to the Fantasy Floor, *non*?" answered the mouse. "This is the way."

Her brothers nodded. Rose took a deep breath and stepped over the chain.

The hallway was dim, lit only by a medieval-style wall sconce. At the end of the short hall was a single brass elevator bank. Instead of a set of UP and DOWN buttons, there was a panel of multiple buttons, each button corresponding to a letter of the alphabet.

"This elevator can only be opened with a special code," Jacques said. "Each guest decides his or her own."

"What is Lily's code?" Sage asked.

"Je ne sais pas!" said Jacques. "I just waited here in the corner until a bellhop called the elevator, then darted in after him. He was bringing the famous woman her caviar."

"Did you see how many buttons the bellhop pressed?" Rose asked.

Jacques thought a minute. "I think. . . he pressed five buttons."

Rose thought a minute.

Ty was shaking his head. "I don't get it," he said. *"TIABLO* is six letters."

As Sage stifled a laugh, Rose held her finger above the buttons, took a deep breath, then typed in *B O O K E.*

A lamp above the elevator lit up, a bell dinged, and the elevator doors slid open. Ty patted Rose on the back. "Nice one, *mi hermana*."

"Guess Lily's got the Cookery Booke on the brain," said Sage as they stepped inside.

The elevator itself contained only one button, numbered 17.

"But there are only sixteen floors in this hotel!" said Rose.

"Or so you *thought*," said Jacques.

Rose pressed 17. The doors closed, and the elevator rumbled as it ascended to the secret floor. After just a moment or two, a bell dinged, and the doors opened into a small antechamber with a door on each wall.

"Through that door," whispered Jacques, pointing with one little claw at the door opposite the elevator.

Rose padded across the room, then jiggled the doorknob of the main room; but the door wouldn't budge. "It's locked!"

Ty groaned. "Why didn't you tell us we needed a key?" he asked Jacques.

Jacques was fretfully chewing on his tail. "The witch woman opened the door for the bellhop. I never saw a key."

Rose sighed as Sage knelt down in front of the doorknob. "Look!" he whispered. "There's a keyhole!"

Rose knelt next to her brother. Sure enough, under the door handle was a keyhole large enough to actually see through. The door to the Bliss family suite used a modern keycard lock. Rose figured it must have been part of the charm of the Fantasy Floor that the doors used the large, old-fashioned metal keys that Rose had only seen in movies and read about in books.

Sage was peering through the keyhole. "I can see the Booke!"

Rose shouldered Sage aside and put her eye to the keyhole.

The light inside Lily's suite was dim, but Rose could make out a lavish living room with a grand piano and a purple velvet ottoman bigger than a normal person's mattress.

Lying on top of the ottoman was the Cookery Booke, and lying next to it was the Shrunken Man, who seemed to be Lily's assistant.

"My turn," said Ty, pushing Rose out of the way. But when Ty looked through the keyhole, he was so startled by the Shrunken Man on the ottoman that he scrambled back from the door, accidentally knocking his head on the knob.

"Who *is* that little guy?" he cried.

"I told you there *was* a little man talking to Lily!" Rose said as she dropped back to the keyhole. What she saw made her fall back from the door as quickly as her brother had. The strange little man was sitting up and looking right at her, his eyes glowing the same unearthly shade of green they had before in the expo centre when he'd stared right at Rose.

As Rose struggled to her feet, Jacques spilled out of her shirt pocket and tumbled across the floor. Rose grabbed her brothers by their collars and hauled them to the elevator. "Press the Down button!" she hissed. "Hurry!"

Ty smacked his hand against the Lobby button, and they all looked up at the light above the elevator, silently pleading. Behind them, Rose could hear footsteps crossing to Lily's door.

Rose glanced back to see what had happened to Jacques. He was shaking his head.

"Jacques!" Rose hissed. "Are you coming?"

"Surely you jest!" screamed the little mouse. "I am never coming near you people again!"

Just then the knob on Lily's door started to turn. Without a backward glance, Jacques scampered through a hole in the floor.

"I don't want to die!" Sage cried, curling up behind Rose.

The elevator dinged, the light came on, and Rose and her brothers piled inside. They turned to see the Shrunken Man hurtling across the antechamber, reaching for them with a pair of tiny, clawed hands.

And then the doors hissed closed.

Chapter 7

PICTURE IM-PERFECT

THE NEXT MORNING, Jean-Pierre entered the expo hall resplendent in his usual red-velvet chef's coat.

"What you've all been waiting for – today's category! I've issued this particular theme several times before, and it always yields interesting results. The theme is... SOUR!"

SOUR was last of the possible categories they'd listed the night before, and Rose doubted that Balthazar had made it all the way through to the end of the list with his translations.

When Rose looked over to Lily's kitchen, her brow furrowed even more. The Shrunken Man was standing outside the circle of cameras, glaring at her. He smiled, then mimed a knife with his finger and dragged it across his tanned neck.

"Ty!" Rose whispered. "Did you see that? The little man just issued an official death threat!"

Ty looked over at Lily's kitchen. "Who, Rumpel-stupids-kin? I could literally step on that guy. Jacques could swallow him. Gus could hiss and the guy would think Al was a sphinx. It's ridiculous."

Ty looked over at the Shrunken Man and mimed putting him in a headlock.

The Shrunken Man just kept smiling as he pulled out a tiny vial of glowing violet liquid. He mimed drinking the liquid, then sank dramatically to the ground.

I should never have roped Ty and Sage into trying to steal back the Booke, Rose thought.

Just then Purdy, Balthazar, and the rest of the family rushed up to them.

"Well, we know exactly what Lily will be preparing," Purdy said, brandishing a miniature copy of the final list. "Sourpatch Pie."

Balthazar stuck his tongue out. "Ugh. Capers in a pie. No one wants that. When people ask for something sour, they always want it tempered with something sweet, even if they can't articulate it."

Purdy nodded sagely. "That's right. So according to the list, we settled on a. . . Double Orange Whoopie Pie. Balthazar, do you think you'll be able to translate the recipe within the hour while we go get our magical ingredient?"

"No need!" he said, pulling a sheet of paper triumphantly from his pocket. "I always work backward from the end of a list. SOUR was the first recipe I translated last night. Here it is. The best part is that the magic ingredient is right here in Paris." He slammed the paper down on the chopping block, and Rose took a look at the recipe:

Double Orange Whoopie Pie,
By All Accounts, the Sweetest and Sourest Confection
ever Assembled.

It was in 1671, in the Italian city of FLORENCE, that Signora Artemisia Bliss did manage to spare her own head by creating a dessert that pleased both the ruthless Duke Alessandro di Medici and his ruthless wife, the Duchess Margareta. Alessandro did prefer sweet desserts, and Margareta, sour. Signora Bliss, the Court Baker, was ordered to create a wedding dessert that would please both the Duke and the Duchess, on Pain of DEATH. The fearsome rulers did spare her life upon sampling her double orange Whoopie pie.

Signora Bliss did create two cookies of orange by mixing together the flesh of one PUMPKIN, one fist of WHITE FLOUR, one of the CHICKEN'S EGGS, and one fist of SUGAR.

She did bind the cookies together with a frosting wrought from the vigorous mixing of one fist CONFECTIONERS' SUGAR, one staff of BUTTER, the juice of one BLOOD ORANGE, and the SECRET THAT LIES BEHIND THE ENIGMATIC SMILE OF THE MONA LISA, UTTERED BY THE PORTRAIT HERSELF.

Rose gulped. "We need to collect the secret of the Mona Lisa's smile?"

"Looks like it," said Purdy. "You didn't warn us last night, Balthazar, when you suggested the recipe."

"Hey!" he grunted, adjusting his purple cardigan. "You want your stuff to taste the best, you gotta collect the best. There's nothing more sweet-and-sour than the Mona Lisa's smile. Of course, it's a very rare ingredient, and I don't have it in my suitcase. We've got to go straight to the source."

"All right," said Albert, pouring himself a glass of water and gulping it down. "I guess we're off to the Louvre museum."

"Why are we going to a museum *now*?" whined Sage. "I thought the one perk of this non-vacation was that we'd be too busy to go to a museum."

But Leigh shivered with delight. "Art!" she screamed. "Nectar of the human soul!"

The Louvre looked to Rose like a medieval castle – save for the famous glass pyramid in the courtyard. The building was so enormous that at first she didn't realise it was all the same. "How big is this place?"

"Big enough to be seen from space," her father said. "Now come on."

The Blisses hurried to the entrance and found themselves at the back of a line that wound all the way around the block.

"This is worse than Disney World!" said Albert. He poked the shoulder of the uniformed soldier in front of him. "Sir? Do you know how long the wait is?"

"About three hours," said the man.

Purdy looked at her watch. "We only have fifty-two minutes! Are you sure we can't substitute a different ingredient, Balthazar?"

"It *has* to be the Mona Lisa's secret," he answered gruffly. "No way around it." Balthazar had donned a baseball hat that was too big, even for his massive cranium, and had painted his nose and cheeks with pasty white zinc oxide to protect them from the sun.

"I have an idea," Sage announced. "Let's tell the guards that I have a rare disease where I can't be out in the sun. They'll let us in just to spare my life!"

Purdy shook her head. "That's immoral," she said. "Also, that's a real disease. It's called Xeroderma Pigmentosum."

"Huh," pondered Balthazar. "You know, I think the kid is on to something. We oughtta try. We've only got forty-nine minutes."

Balthazar pulled a napkin from his pocket. Inside was a flaky pastry that looked chalky and old. "Here. We all need a bite of this before we get inside. It's a Portrait Pop-Tart. Makes it so you can hear what the folks in the paintings are saying."

Rose took a bite of the Portrait Pop-Tart. It was as dry and hard as a fingernail, and the jelly inside had dried into dehydrated red flakes. "When is this from?" she asked, doing her best not to spit her bite on to the curb.

"Nineteen fifty-five," answered Balthazar. "Sorry about that. I considered making a new one last night, just in case, but I had this perfectly good one stuffed in my suitcase."

As soon as everyone had managed to scarf down a bite of the ancient Portrait Pop-Tart, Sage unwrapped the blue pashmina Purdy was wearing around her neck and draped it over his head, then spread some of Balthazar's zinc oxide on his nose. "Let's go."

Heads turned as the Blisses marched around the block to the front of the line. At the entrance, a tired woman with short brown curls was taking tickets.

"Excuse me, ma'am," said Sage. "My name is Leonardo Da Bliss, and I've travelled all the way here from Alaska with my family."

Sage indicated the motley crew that stood behind him.

"I have a rare condition called. . . zero-drama piggytosis." Sage glanced back at Purdy, who smiled nervously. "I am allergic to the sun. My whole life, all I've wanted was to see the *Mona Lisa*, painted by my namesake, Leonardo Da Vinci. But I can't wait in this line for another three hours under the blazing sun. I was hoping you could let me and my family in, or else I'll have to go back to my hotel and look at pictures of the *Mona Lisa* on the internet."

Rose could barely believe what a whopper of a lie her brother had just told, though she had to hand it to him – he had pulled it off without flinching.

Rose risked a glance at the ticket taker. It seemed to have worked!

The ticket taker smiled gently. "Sure, sweet one. You and your brother and sisters can come in for free. But it'll be thirty euros for the adults. And you'll have to put the cat in the cloakroom."

Balthazar looked like someone had punched him in the stomach. "Thirty euros?" he gasped. "That's forty bucks! Outrageous! Just send the kids in."

While Purdy, Albert, Balthazar, and Gus waited outside, the four kids marched right in to search for the *Mona Lisa*.

Everybody walking through the halls of the Louvre spoke in hushed tones, which was good, because the din coming from the portraits was deafening.

It was impossible, for instance, to ignore the portrait of Napoleon Bonaparte crossing the Alps on horseback. "I've grown weary of our journey," he whined. "My toes are frostbitten. I've changed my mind about Russia – I don't want to go any more. I hear in Russia they put small dolls inside of larger dolls. I don't understand. I can no longer feel my fingers. Does anyone have a slice of quiche? Are we there yet?"

Sage couldn't resist. He walked over to the portrait of Napoleon. "I sympathise, Your Excellency."

Napoleon's eyes seemed to shift ever so slightly to Sage's face. While his mouth didn't move, the Bliss children could hear exactly what he was saying.

"You can hear me?" the portrait asked Sage.

"Yes, sir," said Sage.

"*C'est beau*," whispered Napoleon. "Bring me a croissant! And a carafe of my finest wine! This horse's hair is coarse and unpleasant. Bring me a donkey!"

"It's been a pleasure, sir," said Sage, saluting Napoleon and rejoining the group.

"Wait!" called the painting. "Where are you going?"

"Wow," whispered Sage as he continued down the hallway. "He really *is* a whiner! Can you believe that guy, Ty?"

Ty offered no reply – he was too busy staring at a portrait of a naked woman's back. He managed to look away long enough to read the name of the painter on the card next to the painting. "Jean-Auguste-Dominique Ingres," he said. He turned back to the painting. "*Hola, mi amor*. Is that the name of your. . . husband? Your boyfriend?"

While the woman in the painting didn't move, Rose could clearly hear her voice. "He was just a guy I met at the market while I was buying beans," she said. "He told me this painting was just for practice. He said people thought he was a terrible artist and no one would ever see it. But here we are, well over a century later, and a thousand different people stare at my butt every day. You among them."

Ty blushed. "I'm sorry," he said, looking at the floor.

They hurried on.

Rose elbowed her brother. "Serves you right for trying to pick up someone in a painting."

At the end of the hall, a crowd of tourists stood in a huddle, all facing the wall. Rose stood on her toes and strained to see what they were looking at.

There she was: the Mona Lisa.

The painting was much smaller than Rose had

pictured. It was covered by glass and illuminated from above by a small lamp. Rose squeezed her way to the front of the crowd to hear what the Mona Lisa was saying, but the painting was silent.

"Hello," Rose whispered. "Mona?"

Nothing – except for confused stares from the people standing next to her.

"Let's let the strange little girl have her moment alone," whispered one couple.

The crowd that had gathered around the portrait dispersed when they heard Rose whispering to herself. Before long, Rose and her brothers found themselves face-to-face with the famous portrait.

"I said, Hello!" Rose whispered again.

"Oh, I heard you the first time," the painting said, her voice soft and low.

"I. . . we. . . we are in a baking competition," Rose whispered to the painting. "We need to capture the secret of your smile. So, if you'll just tell us, we'll be on our way."

The painting scoffed. "Everyone thinks I'm smiling. I'm not smiling! I'm frowning, like a respectable woman. So, whatever you need for your baking competition, you'll have to find it somewhere else."

Chapter 8

MAKING WHOOPIE

"I GOT THIS," Ty said, running his fingers through his hair. He sauntered up to the painting, bit his lower lip, and furrowed his brow in a pose that Ty had practised many times and called 'The Album Cover.'

"You look like you are having surgery," said the Mona Lisa.

Ty broke his pose and let out his breath. "What do you mean? I practised that face for two days! I did so much research!"

"I hate to break it to you," said the painting, "but you look like—" and then she said things Rose had never heard an adult woman say before in her life, let alone a painting of an adult woman.

Ty gasped. "You have a dirty mouth! No wonder you keep it closed!"

Rose turned to look for Leigh, who'd wandered down the hallway and was having words with a docent who wore a red uniform that made him look like a bellhop.

"I just wanted you to know that your biography of Eugène Delacroix contains glaring misinformation," Leigh argued, scratching a bit of spilled oatmeal off the front of her crusty *101 Dalmatians* T-shirt. "Though he did in fact attend both schools, it was at the Lycée Pierre Corneille that he first won accolades for his illustrations and not at the Lycée Louis-le-Grand as your placard asserts."

The docent looked around wildly, wondering if he was the subject of a hidden-camera show, as the young woman who knew the details of Delacroix's biography looked no more than four.

"Leigh! Get over here!" called Rose.

"I'm in the middle of something," she answered.

"I will be in the middle of a nervous breakdown, Leigh, if you don't come back here right now."

Leigh begrudgingly toddled over to Rose and Ty and Sage.

Why am I the only one who can behave like a normal person? Rose wondered.

"Well, well, well. If it isn't Mrs Lisa Giocondo herself," said Leigh, her tiny arms crossed coolly over her chest.

"Her name is *Mona Lisa*," Rose corrected.

"No, the little one got it right," the painting said. "My name is Mrs Lisa Giocondo. *Mona* means 'ma'am,' and yet everyone always calls me Mona. It's not a name!"

Rose was speechless. "I didn't know. I'm sorry." Rose turned to Ty and whispered, "Why is this woman so crabby?"

"I heard that," said Mona Lisa. "I'm two-dimensional, not deaf."

"No need to apologise for being crabby," said Leigh. "You'd be crabby, too, if you were subject to the Byzantine gender politics of the sixteenth-century Florentine upper class. Lisa here was born in the late seventies – *fourteen seventies*, that is – and when she was fifteen or so – just a couple of years older than you, Rose! – she was forced to marry a man in his forties, then proceed to raise six children. Am I right?"

Now the Mona Lisa was speechless. "Go on," she finally said.

"She wasn't expected to have any interests of her own, except for cleaning and cooking, and she rarely left the house, except to sit for twelve hours straight in Leonardo Da Vinci's studio because her husband wanted to have a picture of her."

"You're making this worse, Leigh," said Rose. Rose pulled a pacifier from her pocket and popped it into Leigh's mouth.

"Take that little plastic giblet out at once!" cried the painting. "This child is the only one who understands me! Please, young soothsayer. Continue."

Leigh spat out the pacifier and cleared her throat. "I've watched all the art criticism about the enigmatic 'half smile' of the *Mona Lisa* on the Art History Channel, but I personally have always thought you were simply trying *not* to smile. Renaissance portraiture consists exclusively of sour, pious frowns. You were trying your best to maintain a frown, but something in the room tickled you, something—"

"There was something," the painting said.

"Sage," Rose whispered. "Get the jar out!"

Sage removed a miniature mason jar of tinted blue glass from the side pocket of his cargo trousers and held it near the painting.

"I'm guessing it was something you saw in Leonardo's studio," Leigh continued.

"It was the flying machine!" said the painting. Her

voice soared in a lilting soprano. "When I was a young girl, living on Daddy's farm, I was charged with looking after the hens. There were twelve of them, all cooped up in a pen, forced to lay egg after egg, never allowed to roam free. I always wondered why they never tried to fly over the fence. I thought perhaps it was because they were afraid they'd be caught."

"Are you getting this?" Rose whispered to Sage.

Sage nodded.

"My favourite hen was a red one that I called Lisa. After myself. One night, I snuck into the hen coop and stole Lisa from her cage. I placed her in an open meadow, under the moonlight. 'Fly away, Lisa!' I cried. 'Fly away!' She tried. But chickens are too large and too clumsy to fly. She only made it a few feet. I had to bring her back to the coop."

Sage was straining to hold up the jar, which had begun to overflow with a dense, brown paste the consistency of refried beans.

"I think we have enough," said Sage, spilling paste on to the floor as he fastened the lid on the jar. "Thank you, Lisa."

"I'm not finished! Open that jar!" Lisa cried. With a nod from Rose, Sage reluctantly opened the jar.

"After that," the painting continued, "I married Francisco and delivered child after child. I thought of Lisa the chicken, laying egg after egg. Though I loved my children more than life, I yearned for the freedom of the swallow. But I was as clumsy as Lisa the chicken, unable to escape!

"Francisco commissioned a portrait from the great Leonardo Da Vinci. Imagine my shock as I sat down in his studio only to see a noble, perfect flying machine sitting in the corner! He told me to frown as piously as I could, but all I could think of was getting in that flying machine and flying away."

"I think the paint fumes have gotten to her brain," whispered Ty.

"And so I smiled fancifully the whole time that Leonardo painted as I dreamed of flight."

"Thank you!" said Sage, fastening the lid once more. "What a tale! Let's go, guys. This thing weighs more than Leigh does."

Rose and her brothers began to back away from the painting, jar and Leigh in tow.

"Stay!" she cried. "Stay and hear about the time I accidentally broke my leg as I attempted to fly from the roof of my porch!"

"Another time!" yelled Rose as she hurried her siblings out of the Louvre. "Not bad, Leigh," she whispered, thankful that her brothers and sister had been there to help.

By the time Rose and Ty made it back to their kitchen in the Hôtel de Ville expo centre, the baking hour was already under way.

"We've lost six minutes, Ty!" Rose huffed. "We have to hurry!"

Rose scurried to the pantry to pick out her ingredients, visualising the particular look of Balthazar's calligraphy as she remembered the measurements for the pumpkin cookies and blood orange frosting.

The hour of competition flew by as Rose and Ty mixed the pumpkin cookie dough in one bowl and the tart blood orange frosting in another. They added a scant teaspoon of the Mona Lisa's secret to the frosting, which made the bowl levitate and spin like Leonardo's flying machine. Rose and Ty managed to pounce on the bowl and hold it down on the table before anyone could notice the momentary breach in the laws of physics.

When Rose and Ty pulled the cookies from the oven,

they had just one minute to smear frosting on to the pair. Rose was so busy that she forgot all about Lily until after the wall timer had rung and Jean-Pierre Jeanpierre was approaching.

Rose looked around the room as if for the first time that day.

The kitchens from the ten contestants eliminated the day before had been dusted in mounds of flour and lay barren and white, like villages covered in volcanic ash. Across the room, Lily had placed her Sourpatch Pie on her kitchen table. Steam rose from the perfectly browned pie in little waves, like an illustration in a children's book. Lily glanced at Rose's whoopie pies and smirked, as if Rose were offering up cans of cat food.

Rose hated to admit it, but Lily's pie looked perfect. She stared down at her own creation, which was the shape of a tennis ball and the colour of a bad prom dress. It wasn't the most sophisticated-looking dessert, but it contained the secrets of the *Mona Lisa*.

Whatever happens, she thought, *I know I couldn't have tried any harder.*

Marco wielded his long silver cart as he pranced down the black-and-white aisle, loading the ten remaining contestants' desserts on to the tray and delivering them to Jean-Pierre's judge's table on the stage at the front of the room.

Flaurabelle escorted Jean-Pierre to his seat. "After I taste these ten desserts, only five contestants will remain. *Bonne chance.*"

Jean-Pierre tasted plate after plate, nodding in obvious approval or disgust. He seemed to enjoy Rohit Mansikhani's Tart Blackberry Tart so much that he nearly fell back in his chair. He winked at Lily after eating a slice of her Sourpatch Pie. He smiled after eating Dag Ferskjold's Lemon Panna Cotta, he rubbed his belly after sipping Wen Wei's Bitter Chocolate Mousse, and he winced in horror after taking a bite of Miriam and Muriel Desjardins's Key Lime Cupcakes.

"Vile," he whispered, after which the twins threw their arms around each other and each sobbed on a shoulder pad of the other's chic blue blazer.

The last plate in Jean-Pierre's line was Rose's Double Orange Whoopie Pie.

"Is this. . . real?" He removed his spectacles and rubbed his eyes, then put the glasses back on. "Yes, it appears it is! Someone has made an orange ball. At the Gala des Gâteaux Grands. What do you call this thing, young lady?"

"It's a *Double Orange Whoopie Pie.*"

Jean-Pierre turned to Flaurabelle. "Remind me to put a limit on the age of our entrants next year. No one under thirty." Jean-Pierre lifted the whoopie pie, eyed it doubtfully, and then took a bite. His eyes went wide. He shoved the entire thing into his mouth and gulped.

"It's. . . I don't know what it is. . . ," he said. "There's an ineffable quality, an elusive something or other. It holds a secret. Perfectly sweet and perfectly sour at the same time. It makes me feel. . . confused. In the best way. I like this *whoopie pie* very much."

Jean-Pierre looked straight into Rose's eyes. "I look forward to seeing what you'll create *tomorrow*. Yes, everyone, Rose Bliss survives to cook another day, along with Chefs Lily Le Fay, Wen Wei, Dag Ferskjold, and our winner, Roshni Mansukhani. The rest of you may return to your sad little lives."

Rose blushed as Ty did a gyrating victory dance, then glanced over at Lily, who was smiling tersely. Unlike Mona Lisa, who tried to frown but couldn't help smiling, Lily tried to smile but couldn't help fuming.

That afternoon, Albert took the whole family out for victory omelettes at a small, dark café. Rose hadn't won. But neither, unexpectedly, had Lily.

Rose sat at one end of the long, rectangular table, flanked by Ty and Sage and Leigh, while Albert and Purdy and Balthazar sat at the other end of the table.

Albert cleared his throat, stood, and clanged his knife against his water glass.

"Everyone did a great job today," he said. "But we need to start preparing for the rest of the week immediately. Your mother and I will collect ingredients from the top of the list – that's PUFFED, FILO, CHEESY, and CHOCOLATE – and the kids will collect ingredients from the bottom – that's AIRY, SUGARLESS, FLAKY, and ROLLED."

"I already translated the recipes for all the kids' categories but one," said Balthazar. "Since I work my way from the bottom and all. They're back at the hotel."

"I suggest we start collecting now. We have limited time, and some of these ingredients are very hard to come by," Purdy said.

In the hotel suite, Balthazar handed Rose three sheets of paper, each printed with a different magical recipe. Albert and Purdy left to collect the magical ingredient in the Nectar-of-Joy Cream Puffs in case Jean-Pierre announced the PUFFED category the following morning.

Rose sat on the couch with Ty and Sage and Leigh, holding the stack of three recipes. She examined the first of the stack, the AIRY recipe for Angel's Breath Food Cake.

Angel's Breath Food Cake,
for the Appearance of a Dessert
when really there is none.

It was in 1322, in the Japanese fishing village of Hamamura, that Chef Hiroshi Bliss did manage to cure the portly councilman Aki Mayuchi of his dangerous addiction to white cake. Councilman Mayuchi did eat vanilla cake on no less than fourteen occasions per day, which made him larger than the town's largest sumo wrestler. Chef Bliss did create this Angel's Breath Food Cake, which did look like an exact replica of Councilman Mayuchi's beloved white cake, but did contain 90 per cent air instead. Councilman Mayuchi continued to eat fourteen of the cakes per day, but he did return to his normal size, unaware that the cakes were made of air.

Chef Bliss did combine two-and-one-half fists of FINE WHITE FLOUR, two fists of SUGAR, the WHITES OF SIX CHICKEN'S EGGS, and a single GHOSTLY GUST.

The recipe went on to spell out the baking time and temperature, but Rose couldn't get past that final ingredient.

"A *ghostly gust*?" said Rose, pacing over to Balthazar's room. "Balthazar? What's a ghostly gust?"

"I'm busy translating!" he grunted, shutting the door. "Ask the cat. He knows all about gusts."

"What are you implying?" Gus snapped back. Then the cat dashed out from Balthazar's room just before the door slammed shut and hopped up on to the couch. "A ghostly gust? Why, a ghostly gust is simply a wish."

"That's easy enough," Sage said. "I've got *tons* of wishes."

"I wasn't finished." Gus flicked his tail. "It's the wish. . . of a ghost."

Chapter 9

A GRAVE BIRTHDAY CELEBRATION

"A GHOST?" ROSE gasped. "Wait. Ghosts are real?"

"Oh, certainly!" Gus replied. "And there's nothing airier than a ghostly gust."

Leigh yawned heavily. "I shan't concern myself with such foolishness. I am going to take a break from the tedium of the world in the hairy arms of Morpheus!"

"What is she talking about?" said Ty.

"That was Leigh's pretentious way of saying that she is going to take a nap," Gus said. "Even *I* thought it was pretentious, and that's saying a lot."

As Leigh toddled off to her bedroom, Gus began again. "As I was saying, ghosts are quite real."

"How do you know?" asked Sage. "Have you ever seen a ghost?"

"Oh, several times," the cat said, his tail stretched

high in the air like the pole at the back of a bumper car. "Ghosts often come to Mexico to unwind."

"Wouldn't it be more of a sure bet," Rose whispered, "to just try to sneak into Lily's suite again? Ghosts don't sound very reliable, and we need the Booke back. There's too much at stake."

"I want to meet a ghost! Let's bust out of here and find one!" Sage swept Gus off the ground and planted the cat on his lap. "Ah. . . where are we busting *to*?"

"I can't help you there," Gus said, an ear tacked to either side of his head. "My second wife, Reiko, is a ghost, but she currently resides in Japan."

Ty swivelled away from the mirror above the couch, where he was fixing the front-most spike of his red hair. "Can't we just go to a haunted house or something?"

"That's not the way it works," said Gus, rolling over on to his back. "A ghost chooses whether he or she wants to be seen. You've got to know where a ghost lives, pay a visit, ring the bell, bring a gift. It's like going to someone's apartment. But I don't know the address of any French ghosts."

"I bet Jacques does!" Sage cried. "He's from Paris; maybe he had a mouse friend who's now a ghost or something."

Rose sat on the couch with her hands folded politely over her jeans. "I don't think Jacques likes us much. Plus, our brilliant feline friend *Gus* told him never to come back."

Gus flopped on to the floor and commenced licking his thigh. "I was only following the code set down in the *Book of the Scottish Fold*."

"Maybe, but right now we need Jacques to come back," said Rose. "So I'm asking you politely to stop cleaning your thigh and undo your warning."

Gus began nipping at the bottom of one of his hind feet. "I might consider it," he said between bites, "if I knew where he was lurking."

Rose bounded into her room and crouched under the antique writing desk where Jacques lived. She could hear the faint sound of flute music. "Jacques? Did you hear all that?" she whispered.

The music stopped. "*Mais oui*," came a pathetic voice.

"I'm so sorry about dropping you when we were up on the Fantasy Floor," Rose said. "I promise that will never happen again. Can you ever forgive me?"

"Of course I can," said the quiet little voice. "I am usually not one for adventure. I am but a humble musician. Yet you have inspired me. I do, indeed, know a ghost, and I can take you to him. But first, the fanged one must rescind his warning."

"It's your lucky day, Gus," Rose said. "I found Jacques! Now get over here and rescind your warning."

Holding his head high and his puffy tail higher, Gus made his way across the Persian rug to the baseboard underneath the antique writing desk in Rose's room. Looking away from the hole, he stiffly said, "As much as it pains me to say this, I formally rescind my warning. You may enter."

Jacques stepped out of the hole holding his silver flute. He held the flute at one end, like a rapier, and pressed the other end to the tip of Gus's nose. "I formally accept your rescinding," the little mouse said, "on the condition that you never tell any of my relatives how foolishly I am acting by entering this suite again."

"I won't tell yours if you won't tell mine," Gus murmured. The two creatures looked each other in the eye, then the mouse nodded and lowered his flute. The cat extended one of his claws and presented it to Jacques, who grasped the claw with both of his paws and shook it up and down once.

"Great," said Rose, tapping on her watch. "Now, where's that ghost friend of yours, Jacques?"

"I will take you to him. We will need to bring a cake, and candles."

Ty shone a flashlight down the dank, narrow staircase of the Catacombs of Paris.

"Be careful," said Jacques. He was nestled comfortably in the pocket of Rose's hooded sweatshirt, which was just big enough to fit the body of a tiny mouse. "The stones in these steps are very old and very slick, from the countless hordes of people who have trod upon them over the centuries."

Rose kept one hand on her brother's shoulder and followed Ty to the bottom of the dark stairs. Rose was carrying a mini chocolate cake and a carton of birthday candles and a box of matches. Sage was right behind her, carrying Gus.

Rose shivered. The hallway before them was narrow and the ceilings were low. Water dribbled down the walls and puddled on the floor. The Catacombs were about as warm as the walk-in refrigerator at the Bliss Bakery. Rose pulled her sweatshirt tighter against her. She had never even liked *above*ground graveyards, so she had been less than thrilled to hear that Jacques's ghost friend lived in a graveyard beneath the streets.

Ty, on the other hand, counted *Pet Sematary* as his favourite film and was thrilled to be venturing into a catacomb. As they walked single-file down the hall, he said, "Oh man, Jacques. This is like, the *casa de los muertos*. Too radical, mouse-man. But where are all the graves?"

Rose and Jacques squeezed through a narrow opening at the end of the stone hallway. "There are no graves," Jacques said quietly. "Just bones."

Through the narrow entrance was a small room where the walls were made entirely of bones. Long, musty thigh bones stacked on top of one another formed a honeycomb pattern, with countless human skulls dotted throughout. On the other side of the room, another corridor, also lined with human bones, led deeper into the Catacombs.

Ty stood frozen in the middle of the room. "Where did they get all these bones?" he whispered in horror.

Sage put Gus down, then pulled his tape recorder from his back pocket and whispered nervously into the microphone. "I guess this is what happens when you hire a coroner as a decorator."

Rose looked at him and rolled her eyes.

"What?" he replied. "I'm using humour to diffuse the tension in here."

Gus seemed unimpressed by the bones. He was more concerned with keeping his paws out of the puddles of water, and he snarled as he shook a stray drop off the tip of his tail. He glared at the mouse, who was still huddled inside the pocket of Rose's sweatshirt. "Were you born here, Jacques?"

"*Zut alors, non!*" Jacques blustered. "I was born in a beautiful village in Aix-en-Provence. I lived here in the Catacombs just after I graduated from music school."

"Why *ever* would you move away from such a sunny place?" Gus said drily.

Jacques went on, ignoring the feline sarcasm. "My neighbour was a ghost named Ourson. He was a good man, but be warned: When he shows himself, do not mention the French Revolution. He's still a bit touchy about that."

They all nodded. Jacques pulled out his tiny flute and played an upbeat little tune that Rose recognised as 'Frère Jacques.'

"I changed my mind!" screamed Ty. He retreated into a corner, his arms raised in a kung fu pose. "I don't want to meet the ghost!"

Jacques straightened his rumpled whiskers. "It is too

late," he said. "I just rang his doorbell – figuratively, of course."

Rose wanted to run from the haunted catacomb just as badly as Ty, but she wanted the Booke back even more, so she stood her ground.

Having found a dry patch on the stone floor, Gus was sitting with his tail tucked around his paws. "Young Rose, you needn't worry. The ghost can't hurt you. Think of him as if he's nothing more than an old, faded photo."

Rose took a deep breath and smiled her thanks at the grey fur ball squatting at her feet.

Rose had shivered when she entered the Catacombs, but she began to realise it was growing colder still, so cold that her breath turned to vapour. Even Gus's faint breath had turned to a steady stream of smoke.

"Jacques!" someone cried.

Rose turned. Standing in the corner – as if he'd been there the whole time and Rose simply hadn't noticed – was a man about twenty-five years old. He was wearing trousers, a waistcoat, and a newsboy cap. Gus had been right – he looked just like a walking, talking cutout from a faded sepia-toned photograph, the kind her parents kept framed in the secret closet behind the walk-in refrigerator at home.

"*Mon petit ami!*" the man said, his words echoing as if he were yelling from far away. "You return!"

"We came to celebrate your birthday, Ourson," said Jacques.

"Ah!" said Ourson, raising his hand to his heart. "And you bring friends!"

Ourson started across the room towards them. While he appeared to walk, his movement was more like floating than footsteps.

"Hello," Rose squeaked. "We, um, brought cake."

Giggling nervously, Sage grabbed the candles and matches from his sweatshirt pocket. He plunged the candles into the cake. His fingers were trembling so hard it took him three tries to light a match. "We're from America," he babbled as he moved the flame from candle to candle. They had managed to scrounge up five. Jacques had told them the number of candles didn't matter. Like many ghosts, Ourson didn't remember things clearly and began each day thinking it was his birthday.

"We are visiting Paris for a baking competition," Sage continued. He giggled. "You know, baking? Like this cake! That was baked. Paris is nice. We saw the Seine. We went to the Louvre. If we have time, we're going to visit the Palace of Versailles."

From his seat in Rose's sweatshirt pocket, Jacques looked at Sage sharply. "Monsieur Sage!" Jacques hissed. "Shh!"

The merry smile dropped from Ourson's face. His eyebrows lowered. "Versailles!" The ghost said it like it was a filthy word. "The palace of the rich and the royal. No expense spared! The king and queen stuffing themselves while the people of France starve!"

Jacques's whiskers wilted. "I warned you."

"We won't stand for it!" the ghost continued. "We will fight—"

Rose shoved the cake with the burning candles in front of Ourson's face, while Sage held the blue jar over the candles.

"Don't you see?" the ghost was saying. "We fight for the dream that is France! *Liberté, egalité, fraternité!*"

Ourson paused and seemed to notice the cake and candles for the first time. His eyebrows lifted, and the smile returned to his face. "Ah," he said. "Lovely." He filled his lungs, puckered his lips into an O, and funnelled a slow stream of ghostly air across the candles. As the flames guttered and went out, Sage angled the jar to catch the ghostly breath, then flipped the lid closed. Sage stared sideways at the jar, then took his hands away. The ghostly gust was so light that the jar hung suspended in air.

"My friends," Ourson said quietly, "shall I tell you what I wish for?"

"Freedom for France?" Rose hazarded. "Death to tyrants?"

"*Non, ma petite amie*," Ourson said with a smile. "I wish for a birthday party. I am angry at Louis the Sixteenth and the architects of the *ancien régime* for so long that I forget how to have a nice time. And so I wish for a party, to remember how. The best part is, my wish comes true, even before I make it. I cannot thank you enough, my friends, for helping me to remember. Thank you."

Rose smiled at the flickering ghost, her fear dropping away as he smiled back. Behind her, Ty whimpered piteously. "Can we go now?"

Back at the Hôtel de Notre Dame, Rose tucked the blue mason jar with the ghostly gust under her bed. She patted Jacques's little body, no bigger than a Ping-Pong ball, which was still tucked into the front pocket of her sweatshirt.

By that time it was nine o'clock. It had been a long

day, what with collecting the Mona Lisa's smile, baking the Double Orange Whoopie Pie, and collecting the ghostly gust. Rose felt like she could barely stand up. Still, she wanted to press on.

She paced behind the couch where Ty and Sage had flopped and begun to nod off. Even Gus was having trouble keeping his eyes open.

"So, the next recipe we need to collect for is. . . ," she said, searching for the sheets of paper, "SUGARLESS Better-Than-Anything Banana Bread."

"Are you kidding?" said Ty, covering his face with a throw pillow. "We need a break. Like, until tomorrow."

"Please, Ty? What if SUGARLESS is the category tomorrow morning? I'm going to lose because you wanted to *sleep*?"

Ty grumbled. "Ugh, fine. What do we need to get?"

Rose turned her attention to the sheet and read aloud:

> *Better-Than-Anything Banana Bread,*
> *an ancient treat for the diabetic.*

> *It was in 867, in the Norse settlement of Jarlshof, that Lady Huegrid Bliss did create a banana bread for a nearby*

village of migrant warriors, none of whom could stomach
sugar. The Ruriks, as they were called, suffered so as they
smelled the sweet confections emanating from Jarlshof that
Lady Bliss did create this recipe, which satisfied the diabetic
Rurik tribe's insatiable craving for sweetness.

Chef Bliss did combine two-and-one-half fists of WHITE
FLOUR, the EGG OF A CHICKEN, the mash of three RIPE
BANANAS, and a dash of VANILLA, along with one fist
of UNSPOILED RAINFALL.

The resulting mixture he did place in an oven HOT as—

"Unspoiled rainfall!" Gus interrupted, his ears perking up. "Balthazar used to attach a dozen blue mason jars to the tail of a helicopter and take it up during a thunderstorm just to collect it. But he didn't bring any with him."

"What will *water* do?" Sage asked, rolling over and pressing his face into the back of the couch.

"It's not just water; it's unspoiled rainfall," Gus said. "The closer a raindrop gets to the ground, the more potency it loses. By the time it hits the pavement, it's just a drop of tap water. But when it condenses inside the cloud, a single drop carries the sweetness of an entire colony of bees, or an acre of sugarcane."

"I don't know if you've noticed, *gato*, but we left our helicopter at home," said Ty.

"Yes, Thyme, I am aware of your lack of helicopters," said Gus. "There is another way. It will require unmitigated bravery, cunning, and a willingness to be carried away."

Sage turned around. "Mum says I get carried away all the time."

The rain started falling before they'd left the hotel. Heavy black clouds had obscured the moon and stars, and thick, cold raindrops beat the pavement like little nails.

By the time Rose and her brothers piled into a freight elevator on the ground floor of the Eiffel Tower, they were soaked through despite the raincoats they all wore. Jacques had elected to stay behind, and Balthazar had put Leigh to bed for the night. Purdy and Albert were still out looking for their list of ingredients.

"Are you certain you want to go up to the third deck,

mes enfants?" asked the lift operator, who wore a black bellhop's coat and hat. "It is raining very hard. Everyone else has gone home!"

"We have to go up right now, sir!" Rose cried. This was their best chance to collect the magic ingredient they'd need to win in the SUGARLESS category. After yesterday's small triumph in the arena of SOURNESS, Rose had begun to think that a victory was possible. She wanted to win. She needed to win. She had to do something to make up to her family, to Calamity Falls, to herself for losing the Booke. The desire burned in her like a bellyache. "Please."

The lift operator stared suspiciously at Sage's rounded belly. Sage was wearing a thick yellow raincoat and yellow fisherman's hat, and underneath the raincoat was Gus, strapped into the baby sling and breathing through a buttonhole in the vinyl. As much as he hated to be out in the wet, Gus had explained that his weight would provide necessary ballast.

"What is underneath that coat?" asked the lift operator.

"I'm afraid it's his natural stomach, sir. He subsists on a diet of microwaveable hash browns. Because our parents are always away."

The lift operator squinted suspiciously at Sage, then

shrugged. "Please enjoy the highest deck on the Eiffel Tower. We close in fifteen minutes."

After a quick trip up the lift, the Blisses stepped out on to the top deck of the tower. The metal platform was slick with water, and rain blew in horizontally on a gale of wind. Rose tried to make out the curve of the Seine, but all she could see was black fog.

"All right, little *hermano*, drink up the good stuff," said Ty, handing Sage a thermos full of Helium Hot Chocolate.

Under Gus's direction, Rose had whipped up the syrupy brown liquid on the hotel stovetop before they'd left: milk, cocoa powder, sugar, and a blast from the rare Helium Beetle, an iridescent blue bug that Balthazar kept in a jar in his suitcase.

"What does that bug do?" Rose had asked.

"It expels helium," Gus had said.

"Expels it from where?" Sage had asked suspiciously.

"If you must know, it expels it from both ends," Gus had said as the beetle had let out a satisfied grunt.

"Oh man! Beetle gas!" Sage had chuckled.

But now that he was in the dark rain, the only illumination coming from a set of wandering searchlights, he forgot all about the hilarity of the beetle gas. He stared nervously at the clouds as he sucked down the warm contents of the thermos.

As Sage drank, Ty tied the rope they'd brought with them in a crisscross harness around Sage's chest and waist. "Tug on the rope twice when you've got the rain from the cloud. Cool?"

Sage handed the thermos back to Rose and licked his lips. "Cool," he squeaked. With all the helium he'd drunk, his voice came out sounding like a sped-up record.

"Don't let any rain get inside this jacket!" Gus yelled, his voice muffled beneath the vinyl. "If I feel so much as a drop of water on my delicate fur, I shall become very crabby!"

Ty let go of Sage and played out the rope as Sage floated slowly off the deck and into the dark, wet sky.

"Wait!" he cried. "I don't want to go!"

Rose had a moment of doubt. This was more dangerous than anything they'd ever done, more dangerous even than visiting a ghost in a catacomb. Wasn't Sage more important than beating Lily and recovering the Booke?

"Ty!" she cried. "Bring him back!"

But it was too late. The bottoms of Sage's feet had

already disappeared into the black clouds overhead. The rope whirred through Ty's hands as Sage rose higher and higher. Ty struggled to get a grip on it. "We shouldn't have used nylon rope," he grunted. "This rain makes it *muy* slippery."

Rose held her breath. It seemed to take forever as the wind and rain whipped the tower, but finally the rope jerked in Ty's hands.

Ty reeled the rope back in, hand over hand, until the soles of Sage's feet broke through the clouds, followed by his legs and his yellow slicker-clad belly, and finally his head and hands. Sage held the jar above his head and grinned at them in triumph. "Got it!" he called.

He was just two metres off the deck when Ty bent down to loop the rope around the railing.

But before he could finish, Gus's head popped out of the bottom of Sage's raincoat. "Water!" Gus shrieked. "There's water on my fur!"

The cat twisted and writhed until he released himself from the baby sling carrier and leaped away from Sage and on to a dry patch of the platform. Without Gus's considerable weight to balance the helium, Sage shot up into the sky, and the wet rope whirred out of Ty's grasp.

"I lost my grip!" Ty cried.

"Hellllpppp!" Sage wailed as the rope slithered along towards the edge of the deck.

Rose screamed as the frayed end of the rope rose up in the air to follow Sage into the sky.

Chapter 10

HEAD IN THE CLOUDS

TY LUNGED FORWARD and with his right hand caught the rope while with his left hand he held on to the railing. "I'm losing my grip again!" he said, the rope slipping inch by inch through his wet hands. "Rose, help!"

Rose scrambled on to his back and wrapped her fist around the rope, too. But it was no use: they were too wet, and the rope was too slippery. "I can't hold it!" she cried.

That's when Gus sprinted out from his dry hiding place and hurtled across the rainy deck. He vaulted over Ty's back, landed on Rose's head, and hooked the rope with one of his claws. "Nothing escapes a cat's clutches!" he announced.

"*Youch!*" Rose cried as Gus dug into her scalp with

the claws on his hind feet. But his hind claws were no match for the Helium Hot Chocolate, and Gus himself began to float upward into the sky, taking some of Rose's hair with him.

"*Rowr!*" he yowled as he slipped up into the air.

But now Rose and Ty had something to hold on to. Rose reached up and grabbed Gus's tail. "Gotcha!"

Rose, still sitting on Ty's shoulders, pulled Gus towards her by his tail, hand over hand, until she was holding him around his fat belly. She strained and reached up past his claws to grab the rope that held Sage from floating away into oblivion. Gus leaped back down to the ground and landed with a thud.

"Why, oh why, did I ever leave Mexico?" he wailed.

As Rose held tight to the rope, Ty backed away from the railing and sunk to his knees, then bent over, giving Rose enough room to climb down from his shoulders and plant her feet firmly on the ground. She and Ty pulled furiously at the rope, reeling their little brother in bit by bit.

Rose sobbed with relief when Sage finally emerged from the clouds overhead.

When his feet were just an inch above the deck, Ty tied off the rope so Sage couldn't drift away again, and

Rose ran forward and threw her arms around him.

"I'm sorry I made you do it," she said. "That was selfish and stupid of me."

"Eh. . . it wasn't that bad," he replied. He smiled, but even Rose could see he was doing it for her benefit. She hugged him harder.

Bobbing just a few inches above the platform, Sage handed the blue mason jar full of water to his brother, then crossed his arms and glared at Gus, who, now soaking wet, was huddled miserably in a corner by the elevator, nursing his sore tail.

"*Water,* Gus?" Sage squeaked with his helium voice, uncharacteristically serious for a change. "You were going to let me float up to Saturn because of a few drops of *water?*"

With his grey coat plastered to his body, the fat cat looked a lot less fat. "To me, water feels like sulphuric acid. How would you like it if I dripped acid on you?"

Rose glared at Gus.

The cat huffed. "I'm sorry I jumped. I put my comfort before your safety. I suppose I panicked."

A smile flickered across Sage's face. "It's OK," he squeaked. "It's worth it to see you soaking wet! Now, how do I get all this helium out of me?"

"I guess you just gotta let it all seep out," said Ty. Because of the rain, his usually spiky hair had wilted and now hung down to his ears. "It shouldn't take too long. We'll just tie you to the ground for a week or so until you start to droop."

Sage beat his bloated gut with both fists. "I feel like I have gas. Wait! I *do* have gas! All I need to do is –"

"*Eew*, Sage, no!" Rose said, fanning her hand in front of her face. "There has to be another way."

"How about belching instead?" Ty said. "That shouldn't be a problem for you, *mi hermano*. You're a champion burper!"

"Great idea," Rose said. Sage could not only burp the alphabet on cue, but all of the state capitals as well.

Sage opened his mouth and pushed from his stomach, but nothing came out. He tried again. "Albany. Tallahassee. Sacramento," he said. His face scrunched up in frustration. "Oh man. I have belcher's block!"

Gus batted a can of ginger ale towards them. "This might do the trick."

Rose scooped up the rolling can. "Where did you get this?" she asked.

"I crawled inside that vending machine," Gus said,

flicking his bedraggled tail at a glowing machine near the elevator. "I nearly got stuck on the way out. I hope that I have adequately demonstrated my willingness to make myself uncomfortable for your sake, young Sage."

"You're too big to crawl inside a vending machine, Gus," Rose said, trying to envision the cat's bloated stomach squeezing inside the tiny slot at the bottom.

"You're right," he answered. "I bought it."

Rose knelt and patted Gus on the head. "Thank you, Gus. This is very helpful." She handed the can to Sage as Gus climbed back into his waterproof hiding place beneath Sage's raincoat.

"Chug! Chug! Chug!" shouted Ty.

Sage cracked open the can and downed the ginger ale in a matter of seconds. After a moment, he hiccupped once, then twice. Then his jaws were forced open by a hot blast as loud as a rifle salute on Memorial Day.

Ty laughed. "Yes, *hermano*! That was a scorcher!"

Sage had dropped closer to the platform, but he was still floating. Then his mouth opened as wide as the end of a tuba, and he let loose a series of long, reverberating blasts that rustled his lips, blew back

Rose's hair, and seemed to shake the very foundation of the Eiffel Tower.

"*Ay yi yi*," Ty said. "I'm not sure that smells any better than the other option."

"Thank goodness we're alone," said Rose. "This is too embarrassing for words."

That was when Rose heard whispers coming from the far corner of the deck. She turned to find Miriam and Muriel Desjardins, the twin bakers who had been eliminated from the competition earlier that day. They were wearing short black skirts and matching blue blazers. Miriam, whose long hair looked perfect, even when drenched, wore a dainty lace scarf; and Muriel, whose chic hair rivalled even the chicness of Lily's old haircut, wore a red beret. They looked like cut-outs from the pages of a French fashion magazine. Muriel was holding a balloon in the shape of a cupcake.

"Hello," Rose said nervously. "How long have you two been standing there?" Rose asked.

"I'll handle this," Ty whispered to Rose. He sauntered over to the girls. "*Amigas!* The name is Thyme Bliss, but you can call me Ty. Or T-Dog. Call me whatever you want. You'll recognise my sister Rose and me from the Gala, I'm sure."

"Yes, we recognise you," Miriam said as she and her twin sister surveyed the strange scene: Ty and Rose standing on a wet, dark roof, and Sage in a yellow raincoat with the head of a grey cat poking out the top.

"What a surprise!" Ty went on. "And what brings you here on this lovely rainy evening?"

"We're here to say goodbye to the Gala des Gâteaux Grands," said Muriel. "We were eliminated today, and they gave us this crummy balloon as a gift. We came up here to set it free."

"She means 'to throw it away,'" said Miriam. "The real question is, what are *you* doing here?" she asked suspiciously.

As if on cue, Sage let loose with his biggest belch yet, which was so powerful that it caught the rain and blew it the other way.

The two girls stepped back a few paces.

"I guess you heard my little brother," Ty replied. "He has a disease called, uh, winditis, which causes uncontrollable belching. It's very embarrassing, so we came up here in the rain so no one would have to listen to how disgusting he is."

"Hey!" Sage yelled. That final roar had expelled all the

remaining gas. Sage's feet were firmly on the platform, and he was busy untying his rope anchor.

"You'll forgive us, right?" said Ty. And then Ty busted out the most revered of all his poses: 'The Surprised Hair-Swipe.' He raised his eyebrows, bowed his head, and ran his fingers through his damp hair.

But Miriam and Muriel were of a different calibre of woman than Ty was used to at Calamity Falls High, and 'The Surprised Hair-Swipe' seemed to have no effect.

"You came up here in the middle of a thunderstorm so your brother could burp?" Muriel smirked. "Interesting. Though it doesn't explain the cat underneath his raincoat and why he's wearing a rope harness that's anchored to the tower."

"There's something funny about your family," said Miriam. "I can't put my finger on it."

"I know," said Ty. "It's funny how attractive we are. Or . . . me, at least."

"No, that's not it," said Miriam. "We'll leave you alone to finish whatever odd thing you were doing."

"No!" Ty cried. "Stay!"

"*Bonne nuit*," said Muriel.

Rose patted Ty on the shoulder as the Desjardins twins disappeared into the elevator.

"'The Surprised Hair-Swipe' *always* works," he whispered, shell-shocked.

"You'll get 'em next time, *mi hermano*," Rose said.

The next morning, Jean-Pierre Jeanpierre looked out over the hall and said, "And then there were five."

Rose, Lily, Rohit Mansukhani, Dag Ferskjold, and Wen Wei had been stationed at the kitchens closest to the stage. Lily's kitchen remained directly across from Rose's.

"Today's category will require superior technique," Jean-Pierre said. "The theme of the day is AIRY."

Phew! Rose thought of the two blue mason jars they'd added to Balthazar's ingredients suitcase and removed the recipe for Angel's Breath Food Cake from her back pocket. She gave it a final once-over, although she almost knew it by heart, having stayed up much of the night memorising the recipes.

"We've got that one totally covered, *mi hermana*," Ty said.

As the remaining contestants hurried out of the room to collect their special ingredient, or huddled with their teams to discuss recipes, Purdy bustled up. Behind her trailed Leigh and Sage. Sage was carrying

Gus in the baby sling. As usual, Gus did not look pleased at the indignity.

"Your dad and I are only halfway through our list of ingredients to collect," Purdy said, "so we're going to go out now and hunt. Balthazar is still back at the hotel, translating. You just sit tight, keep an eye on Leigh, and we'll be back in an hour to watch you bake." Purdy looked down and noticed the ball of brown fur huddled in Rose's sweatshirt pocket. "Oh, Jacques! You came back! Even though the cat warned you not to! This is true bravery, right here."

"I am a spy, after all," Jacques replied.

"All right," said Purdy. "I'm off." She kissed Rose on the forehead and disappeared through the room's big doors.

Sage, Leigh, and Ty watched Purdy go. Sage instantly began fidgeting, which Gus did not appreciate. "I'm bored," said Sage. "What are we supposed to do for an hour before the bake-off starts?"

Across the black-and-white-chequered aisle, with TV and film cameras still documenting her every move, their Aunt Lily was poring over a sheet of paper, probably the recipe for whatever AIRY dessert she'd planned. At her side was the Shrunken Man, a leather satchel in the shape of a water jug hanging from his shoulder. The bag looked full of something, but Rose couldn't tell whether or not it was the Booke.

Rose thought that could mean that the Booke was alone and unguarded. She could picture it sitting there on Lily's ottoman on the Fantasy Floor, ripe for the taking.

"Let's sneak into Lily's room again and take the Booke back," she said, expecting her brothers to jump at the opportunity for mischief. Of course, Rose herself was never out for mischief. But she doubted her ability to produce the perfect slice of Angel's Breath Food Cake. "What if I mess up? I can't risk losing the Booke forever over a baking mistake. I think we should just go take it back."

"I shan't return to the Fantasy Floor!" cried Jacques.

Ty looked hesitant. "I don't know, *mi hermana*. We only have an hour."

"Besides," Sage added, "you have the recipe for the Angel's Breath Food Cake, and you already have the ghostly gust to go with it. This one's kinda in the bag. Why risk everything right now? We don't even know if the Booke is in the hotel room."

"But what if I'm not qualified to do this!" Rose cried.

"It's too risky to put it all on me – I'm not that good a baker."

"But you *are*, Rose. Besides, how would we even get in?" Sage asked. "Lily and the Shrunken Man aren't going to make the same mistake twice. They know we were there. They know *why* we were there. This time, they'll totally see us coming."

"And how will you ensure that Lily and the tiny one stay put for the duration of the hour?" Gus asked.

Rose looked at her little sister, Leigh, and then at Miriam and Muriel, who were sitting in an opera box on the side of the room, looking bored. She looked over at Lily, who was consulting with the Shrunken Man, then noticed that Lily kept a tall stack of 8-x-11 glossy photos on her table. "I think I have a plan."

"I don't know about this, Rose," Sage said. "Trying to steal the Booke back just seems *wrong*."

"It's my fault that she has the Booke at all," Rose said through gritted teeth. She would have said more, but she was afraid she might cry. Everything that was wrong in her life, everything that was wrong in Calamity Falls – it all came back to Rose's mistake. She'd trusted Lily. Rose would do anything to set things right. "I *have* to get it back."

Ty stared at Rose for a minute. "There's a little vein in your forehead that looks like it's gonna blow, Rosita." He turned to Sage and Jacques. "What the heck, right? Let's give it a whirl. For Rose. So her head doesn't explode."

Rose watched as Miriam and Muriel Desjardins fought their way through the cameras around Lily's kitchen and approached her as she worked at her baking table.

"Lily!" Miriam called. "After we were eliminated from the competition yesterday, we were approached by representatives of the Orphanage of Paris. The children have all requested the same thing for their birthdays: your autograph! We were hoping you could take some time out of your busy schedule to sign. . . oh, two hundred photographs or so!"

Lily glanced up, a look of irritation crossing her face. Then she remembered that she was surrounded by cameras. Almost magically, her frown turned into a gleaming smile. "Of course!" she lilted, right into the cameras. "*Anything* for orphans."

Lily pulled a Sharpie marker from her apron and set to work autographing glossy photographs of her glossy face – two hundred of them, to be exact.

"I don't think Lily and the Shrunken Man will be

going anywhere for the next hour," Ty said. "Good idea, *mi hermana.*"

"Thanks," Rose said. "Was it hard to get Miriam and Muriel to do it?"

Ty's grin grew wider. He primped his spiky hair. "Nope. They were suspicious, of course. They wanted to know why I was asking them to do such a strange thing. I told them it was a top-secret mission, and they got even more suspicious. But then I used a one-two punch," he said. "'The Wounded Athlete' look followed by 'The Lost Woodsman.' Never fails."

"How'd you really do it?" Rose asked.

Ty looked sheepishly at the floor. "I gave them fifty bucks."

While Gus and Sage stood vigil in the expo centre kitchen, Ty, Rose, Leigh, and Jacques hurried back to the Hôtel de Notre Dame.

When they got to the lobby, it was time for Leigh to do her part.

"You ready, Leigh?" Rose asked, setting her down.

"If you're assuring me that this is the only way I will ever get to enter the magnificent Lily Le Fay's suite, then yes, I am ready."

Rose and Ty took a seat on a couch by the elevators, with Jacques in Rose's pocket, and watched as Leigh toddled up to the front desk.

"Hello!" Leigh called to the clerk. She banged a fist against the front of the counter. "I have misplaced my key, and I'd like another."

The concierge glanced around in confusion, then leaned over his mahogany desk to see who could possibly be speaking. He was surprised to find a child in a dirty *101 Dalmatians* T-shirt. "Hello there, little one!" the concierge said. "Where's your mother?"

Leigh huffed. "Speak to me with the proper respect, young man! I am a guest in your hotel and a personage of great renown!"

The concierge smiled. "Of course you are. And what room are you in?"

"What room am I in?" Leigh repeated, indignant. "Do not condescend to me, young man! I'm not in a *room* at all! I'm in one of your exclusive suites on the Fantasy Floor!"

"You. . . are?" the concierge asked.

"Oh, this is rich," Leigh announced to the entire lobby. "Do you judge me simply because of my reduced stature? Can no one see past my diminutive form to the sterling mind contained within? No! You are all betrayed by your eyes! No one recognises the Countess Juniper du Frost! The wife of the renowned Count Ashcroft du Frost, assistant to the great Lily Le Fay! I am staying on the Fantasy Floor with my moustachioed husband, in Miss Le Fay's suite, and I have misplaced my key! Kindly please give me another!"

In the sudden silence of the lobby, everyone could hear the concierge swallow. "I am so sorry, Mrs du Frost! It will not happen again." Smiling to the assembled onlookers, he ceremoniously reached down and stuffed an enormous brass key into Leigh's outstretched hand.

Leigh nodded curtly. "That is the level of sublime service I have come to expect in my hoteliers." She bowed and swept her hand wide with a flourish. "I'll see that you receive a commendation from your supervisor!"

Then she spun on her heel and marched back to where her sister and brother waited by the elevator.

She smiled sweetly. "There," she said. "Now get me upstairs. I want to smell Lily's perfume as it permeates the living room."

*　*　*

Moments later, as Rose keyed *B O O K E* into the keypad of the Fantasy Floor elevator bank, she was gripped by a terrible sense of foreboding.

Maybe this is a bad idea, she thought. *Maybe I've gone off the deep end, asking my little sister to pretend to be a famous countess when I'm not even sure the Booke is going to be there. Maybe I've gone too far.*

Ty flicked Rose in the shoulder. "Hey, you OK?"

"Why wouldn't I be?" she snapped.

Rose held her breath all the way up to the seventeenth floor.

Soon the four of them – Rose, Ty, Leigh, and Jacques, in Rose's pocket – stood before the locked door of Lily's suite.

"Jacques," said Rose, "would you mind taking a peek through your hole to make sure there's no one in the room?"

"No problem," said Jacques. He leaped from the pocket of Rose's sweatshirt and scurried across the floor. "Oh no!" he cried once he'd reached the baseboard. "They have plugged up my private entrance!"

"That's not a good sign," Ty said. "How could they have known about Jacques?"

"I'm sure it was the Shrunken Man. A little spy can

173

smell another little spy a mile away," Leigh said sagely as Jacques scrambled up Rose's leg and curled in her pocket once more.

Ty shrugged. "We're here now."

Rose nodded. She slid the key into the lock. "Here goes nothing."

Rose turned the key and swung open the door. Before she could take a single step, however, Leigh ran inside and plopped on to a purple velvet couch sitting next to the ottoman. "That performance has left me utterly drained! Naptime for *moi!*" she announced, promptly falling asleep.

Rose and Ty looked at each other, then crossed to the ottoman where they had spotted the Shrunken Man and the Booke – but the ottoman was empty, save for a small, cream-coloured envelope.

Rose reached down and picked up the envelope.

Immediately, a piercing buzzer rang out.

"What's that, a fire drill?" Ty cried.

Rose pulled a slip of paper from the envelope and read it aloud. "'Surprise, burglars! This is a trap. If you're reading this, then you're about to be on TV! Love, Lily.'"

"What does that mean?" Ty asked.

Even over the piercing wail of the alarm, Rose heard

a rustling in the bedroom. "Quick, hide behind the couch!" she cried. She and Ty hurtled over the back of the purple velvet couch just as a camera crew darted into the living room.

Rose breathed a sigh of relief – until she remembered that Leigh was sleeping in plain view on the other side of the couch.

Chapter 11

BOTHERED, BEWITCHED, AND BEHEADED

A TRAP!

The sofa Leigh had fallen asleep on, and behind which Ty and Rose were hiding, wasn't like a regular sofa at all. It was a long, wrought-iron bench with an intricate filigree pattern covering the back to which purple velvet cushions had been tied. By peering through the spaces between the purple velvet couch cushions, Rose and Ty could see what was going on.

Just after Rose and Ty had leaped behind the couch, three men had run into the living room. They had been lurking in the suite's bedroom, waiting for someone to trip the alarm. The men were dressed in jeans and fleece jackets of various colours. They all had beards. One held a long pole with a fuzzy grey microphone dangling from the end, one carried a hefty camera on his shoulder like a bazooka, and the other – the scrawniest of the three – followed behind with loops of electrical cords dangling from his arms.

Rose crossed her fingers. Maybe the men would think Leigh was an extra-large baby doll and ignore her.

But the man with the hanging microphone lowered it towards Leigh, tickling her ear with its grey fuzz.

As fervently as Leigh loved to nap, she hated to be tickled even more fervently. She bolted up and swatted at the scratchy microphone like it was a swarm of locusts. "Stop, fiend!" she cried.

The fleeced man holding the microphone stumbled backward.

"We—we—we. . . caught you!" he stammered. "We caught you breaking into Lily Le Fay's fantasy suite. What do you have to say for yourself?"

Rose glanced nervously at Ty. Lately Leigh had had a tendency to be too truthful, and in this case, too truthful might get them into serious trouble.

Lie, little sister! Rose wanted to scream. *Lie your head off!*

Leigh was shaking her head in disgust. "Breaking in?" she said incredulously. "Breaking in! That is rich, men. Extra-rich. Nay, nay. Why should I break in when I've got the key?"

Leigh reached into the front pocket of her *101 Dalmatians* T-shirt and pulled out the brass key the concierge had so apologetically handed her just minutes before.

The jaws of the cameraman, microphone man, and wire-wrangler man dropped simultaneously.

"That's right, gentlemen. I am the smallest woman in the world, and I am waiting here for a rendezvous with the smallest man in the world. I was hoping to ease some of the puffiness under my eyes by taking a nap, but since you've so rudely interrupted my regimen of facial restoration, I'll have no choice but to meet my paramour looking like a droopy old sack!

"I see you've been recording the proceedings," Leigh continued, addressing the man with the camera on his shoulder. "If you dare show any of your pitiful 'footage' on television, my lawyer will extract millions of dollars from your low-rent production company and put you out of business."

"We're so sorry, ma'am," the microphone operator said. "It's just, you look like a four-year-old, what with being so small and all, and with your hair and clothes."

"How dare you!" Leigh said. "This weathered *101*

Dalmatians T-shirt was purchased for six hundred dollars at a boutique on Manhattan's Lower East Side. You obviously know very little about style, you—" she pointed to the microphone man "—whose idea of fashion is to carry a pole with a fuzzy grey microphone on it, and you—" she pointed to the wire wrangler "—who thinks loops of wire are the new sleeves."

The wire wrangler hastily gathered together all the loops of cords, unplugged the various machines, and ushered his cohorts out the door. "We do apologise, ma'am."

As soon as Rose heard the *ding* of the elevator from the Fantasy Floor antechamber, she leaped out from behind the couch and hoisted Leigh up in her arms.

"Leigh!" she exclaimed. "You were brilliant!"

Leigh lifted her button nose and patted Rose dispassionately on the cheek without cracking a smile. The old Leigh – before eating the pound cake tainted with Lily's Magic Ingredient – would have melted into Rose's arms and gurgled lovingly, if not eloquently. This new version of Leigh was useful, to be sure, but Rose missed the old one.

Ty patted Leigh on the top of the head, mussing her hairdo, which was like the top of a pineapple.

"Please!" she said, swatting his hand away. "Mind the hair!"

"Watch yourself!" Ty said back. He'd never say it, but Rose could tell he missed his goofy, dirty, unsophisticated little sister as much as she did.

All of a sudden, Jacques popped out from the pocket of Rose's sweatshirt, tapping a nonexistent watch on his wrist. "You must hurry back or be late for the Gala!"

After Ty whipped egg whites in a red bowl, Rose folded in the dry ingredients for the Angel's Breath Food Cake. Then she grabbed the jar with the ghostly gust. Taking a deep breath, she opened the jar over the batter and watched in wonder as the ghost's lighter-than-air wish drifted down and lifted the batter out of the bowl. She punched it back down with a fist, dragged it over the cake pan, and forced it into place. Then she set another cake pan atop it, tied it down with twine, and shoved it into the oven.

"Fingers crossed, Rose," Ty said, forgetting for once to put a Spanish spin on things.

Rose looked across at Lily as she prepared a Springtime Soufflé, a puffy pot of emerald-green fluff that looked to be made entirely of air. The sweet soufflé,

Rose knew, was from the Bliss Cookery Booke, and used the wishes of a growing rosebud to give a person the feeling of springtime even in the dead of winter. Growing rosebuds were shy creatures, and they didn't readily discuss their aspirations, so capturing their wishes was a difficult task indeed. Combined with a dash of Lily's Magic Ingredient, the soufflé was sure to fill Jean-Pierre with a momentary feeling so sublime that he would award her the win for the day.

It just wasn't fair. Lily was guaranteed to win. The thought made Rose so angry that she started across the aisle towards her aunt's kitchen, unsure of what might come out of her mouth when she got there.

She planted her feet across from Lily and tapped her aunt on the shoulder. "Just once," Rose heard herself say, "I'd like to see you try and win without your box of Lily's Magic Ingredient."

Lily stared back at Rose with a look of admiration. She looked almost delighted by Rose's bravery, almost like she wanted to be kind to Rose. Rose recognised the look from when Lily had stayed at their house, before she'd run off with their cookbook. Lily wasn't all rotten, after all. She was a very good baker. And she was lonely.

"Sure," she agreed. "I'll forego the Magic Ingredient. I like your audacity."

Rose walked back to her kitchen, shocked. She hadn't expected Lily to say yes.

Twenty minutes later, Ty pulled the Angel's Breath Food Cake from the oven, and Rose cut a slice and laid it on a plate.

After the giant wall timer dinged, Marco came around and loaded the silver cart with the five AIRY desserts. Rose's stomach turned. Only three contestants would be moving on that afternoon.

Rohit Mansukhani had made a sculpture of Jean-Pierre Jeanpierre's bald head out of white chocolate mousse, which Jean-Pierre seemed to think was both flattering and creepy.

Dag Ferskjold had made a wedding cake covered with coarse black fur. "How does this relate to today's theme, AIRY?" Jean-Pierre asked.

"Airy?" Dag Ferskjold repeated. "AIRY? I thought you said the theme was HAIRY!"

Jean-Pierre reached Wei Wen's plate. He had made some sort of sugary orb that looked to be hollow in the middle. Even though Rose knew the orb wasn't magical, it looked airy enough to give her a run for her money. Jean-Pierre cracked into the orb with a spoon and tasted the fluffy stuff inside.

"*Incroyable!*" he said.

Jean-Pierre moved on to Lily's Springtime Soufflé. He poked at the top of the soufflé, and it sprang back like an expensive mattress.

"I already love it," he gushed.

Let's see what he thinks without all those Lily-loving chemicals, Rose thought.

He took a spoonful of the pale-green cloud and his eyes rolled back in his head. He put down his spoon. "What a phantasm! I feel like I am a young man again!"

Rose's eyes went wide. Jean-Pierre had gone gaga for the dessert without any of Lily's Magic Ingredient.

Jean-Pierre moved on to Rose's plate and stared doubtfully at what she had created.

"A slice of white cake?" he said with a sneer. "First a blackened cookie, then an orange ball, and now a slice of plain white cake?"

But Jean-Pierre's face changed from disgust to wonder as soon as he swallowed his first forkful. "It is. . . so airy!" he exclaimed. "It feels like. . . a ghost! In my mouth!"

"Old family recipe," Rose said with a smile.

Smacking his lips and murmuring, Jean-Pierre waddled back to the stage and his microphone.

"We have, today, a tie. Our winners are Lily Le Fay and Rosemary Bliss! And joining them in competition tomorrow will be Mr Wei Wen."

Rose jumped in the air and threw her arms around Ty. She'd won! Of course, so had Lily – and she'd done it without any of her Magic Ingredient. Rose had to hand it to Lily – she was a great baker. The addition of Lily's Magic Ingredient was a cheat, but her victories were always backed by considerable talent, a talent Rose wasn't sure that she herself possessed.

Rose's parents ran down from the balcony with Balthazar, Sage, and Gus, while Jacques stayed hidden in the front pocket of her sweatshirt, where he'd been hiding the entire time.

"Oh, honey, you did it!" said Purdy, wrapping her arms around Rose. "You were so great."

"Not bad, kids," said Balthazar. "I guess you spent your time before the bake-off really studying that recipe."

"Studying? HAH! The children may speak for themselves. I got to visit Miss Lily Le Fay's hotel suite!" Leigh bragged. "Oh, the luxury! Oh, the resplendence!

What a bright spot in this otherwise dreary so-called holiday I'm having."

"What is she blabbing about?" Purdy asked, suspicious. "Did she go into Lily's room?"

"Um, no!" Rose laughed. "How could she have? You heard Jacques – it's impossible to get into! Maybe the effects of Lily's Magic Ingredient are worsening?"

Purdy's brow lowered, and she looked suspiciously at Rose. "Maybe. At any rate, your father and I have collected what we needed for the FILO Born Yesterday Baklava and the CHEESY Sublime Danish, but we're having difficulty locating a magician's secret for the CHOCOLATE Disappearing Devil's Food Cake. We don't know any magicians here in Paris, let alone ones who are willing to give up a secret."

"You know how magicians are," said Albert. "Greedy."

Albert and Purdy kissed the kids goodbye and went off in search of a loose-lipped magician. By then most of the expo centre had emptied out, and a cleaning crew had descended upon the kitchens.

"We're leaving," said Rose, and she ushered her family down the black-and-white aisle and on to the steps outside the expo centre. The sun had come out in full force after the previous evening's storm.

"I'm still working on the last recipe, the ROLLED Ravishing Rugelach," said Balthazar. "I should have it done by suppertime. How are you kids doing with ingredients for the FLAKY Crazed Croissants?"

Rose pulled out the recipe that Balthazar had written up for the FLAKY category:

Crazed Croissants,
offering Mental Clarity to the disordered.

It was in 1815, in the crowded tenements of London's garment district, that the good lady Larissa Bliss did rescue the hatter John Deveril from the delusions brought on by the mercury fumes that were a hazard of his trade. He had begun to think that his children were characters in nursery rhymes, but after eating one of Lady Larissa's Crazed Croissants, he saw clearly once more.

Lady Larissa Bliss did combine two-and-one-half fists of WHITE FLOUR, the EGG OF A CHICKEN, one fist of WHITE SUGAR, two cups of COW'S MILK, and the BLUSH OF A TRUE QUEEN, DABBED WITH A HANDKERCHIEF.

"The blush of a true queen?" Rose asked, quickly noting the time and temperature for the recipe. "How do we get *that*?"

"Beats me," said Balthazar. "I could never figure out how to get one of those. The only queen I know of lives in England, and I would assume she doesn't let just anyone make her blush."

Rose's shoulders slumped. "This is impossible."

"I have an idea," said Gus.

"The cat has an idea? Since when?" Balthazar asked incredulously. "Usually he just sits around and eats and avoids water."

"I find I can be *very* helpful when I'm appreciated," said Gus. "And I think I know where we can find a queen's blush."

"Pray tell, *gato*," said Ty. "You know a real, live queen? Within walking distance?"

Gus purred. "No one said the queen had to be *alive*."

Rose was a bit annoyed to find herself back in the hall of bones known as the Catacombs of Paris. From the pocket of her sweatshirt Jacques played "Frère Jacques" on his flute; after a moment, Rose felt a chill on the back of her neck. She whirled to find Ourson standing in the corner.

"Ah! My new friends! You return!" said the see-through ghost.

From across the room, Sage and Ty waved nervously. But Leigh strode forward, Gus perched atop her head.

The cat raised a paw to address the ghost. "Hello, ghoul friend!" he said with real warmth and enthusiasm.

"What is this?!" said the ghost. "A cat that speaks? *Merveillieux!*"

"Yes, yes," Gus continued, "I *am* marvellous, I know. But that's not why we're here. We've come back because we need your assistance."

"Anything for my friends!" Ourson replied.

"We need your help contacting a certain. . . non-living person."

"Ah!" The ghost put his hand where his heart would have been. "Who? I have so many friends!"

"You see," Gus explained, "we are in a baking competition. And we need to capture the FLAKIEST thing on this sweet earth, which in my experience happens to be the. . . blush of a queen."

Ourson laughed. "Queens, yes. They do tend towards flakiness!"

"Yes!" Gus said. Rose could tell the cat was nervous, but about what? He'd spoken to ghosts before. "And naturally, we want to capture the blush of the flakiest queen in history, one who happens to reside in Paris. . ."

As Gus went on, Ourson's pallid, sepia-toned face grew pinker and pinker, his strong black eyebrows drew down into a knot, and his upper lip pulled back in a snarl.

Oh no, Rose thought, suddenly understanding why Gus was so nervous.

"And so," Gus finished, "we were wondering if you might happen to know the whereabouts of one. . . Marie Antionette."

At the mention of the name Marie Antoinette, Ourson flew into a rage – literally. The ghost grew big and frightening, his eyes black holes and his mouth wide as he moaned, *"Noooooooooooooooooo!"* He darted around the room of bones, roaring and flitting this way and that until, his rage spent, he sank listlessly to the floor.

From the pocket of Rose's sweatshirt, Jacques shook his fist at Gus. "Fanged One! Creature of Claw and Tooth, how could you? You know how touchy Ourson is about the regime overthrown by the French Revolution! To ask him for the whereabouts of the worst queen in history. . . it is just bad manners!"

With a last glare at the cat, Jacques ducked back into Rose's sweatshirt pocket.

Ourson raised his head up off the ground. "She is incapable of blushing," he said weakly. "She didn't blush when she presided over the starvation of thousands while her wretched husband grew fatter and fatter. Why would she blush now?"

"She is our only hope," Gus said. "We have nowhere else to go."

Ourson dragged his transparent body along the floor like a worm until he reached a wall and could prop his head up against the bones. "She sits on the ledge of the central fountain in the gardens at the Palace of. . ." He stopped, as if choking on the words. "I'm sorry, it still makes me sick to say it."

"Versailles." Gus dipped his head in thanks. "We'll be going now."

As Rose led them out of the room, Jacques called back, "I'm sorry, my friend! I did not know they were going to ask about you-know-who!"

The garden at the Palace of Versailles was a sprawling labyrinth of lawns and flowerbeds that seemed to take up more space than Calamity Falls itself. In the centre of it all was a fountain as big as a baseball diamond, with water jetting from a stack of round tiers like a seven-layer wedding cake.

On their way through the gardens, Leigh stopped to admire a piece of sculpture and couldn't be torn away. "Leave her with me," Ty said. "You can pick us up on the way out."

By the time Rose, Sage, and the animals filed up the main path towards the fountain, it was four in the afternoon, and the sun was bearing down so furiously that most of the visitors had started to trickle towards the exit.

Rose perched on the lip of the fountain as Sage unhooked Gus from the baby sling. She motioned for the cat to join her.

Gus looked mildly taken aback. "Perhaps you've forgotten my adversarial relationship with water? You'll forgive me if I wait over by the DRY shrubs."

Sage sat beside Rose. "When's she gonna come out? Do we have to wait until it's dark? Like with lightning bugs?"

"I'm not sure," Rose answered. "Maybe if Jacques plays something on his flute?"

"Worth a try," Jacques said from her sweatshirt pocket.

He pulled out his tiny flute and piped the familiar strains of the 'La Marseillaise.'

As the last note faded away, Rose felt a cold breeze on the back of her neck. She turned to find a ghost standing in the water, a furious-looking woman with powder-white skin, a toothpaste-white wig of hideous curls, and a frilled dress that pinched her mercilessly at the waist, then puffed out into a skirt as wide as the giant trampoline in the Bliss backyard that Sage loved jumping on.

"How dare you play that revolutionary anthem *here!*" the ghost said.

As nicely dressed as the woman was, there was something odd about her head. It was sitting crookedly on her shoulders. Then Rose remembered how Marie Antoinette had died: she had been beheaded.

The ghost gazed at Rose and Sage, and then spied Jacques leaning out of Rose's sweatshirt pocket.

"A mouse!" she screamed, and disappeared beneath the surface of the water.

"Would you mind sitting this one out?" Rose asked the mouse.

"I am universally despised," Jacques moaned, before ducking deep into Rose's sweatshirt pocket.

After a moment, Marie Antoinette rose cautiously from the water. "Has the mouse gone?"

Ty put a restraining hand on Rose's arm. "Leave this to me," he whispered. "I can make any girl blush." He slipped off his shoes and swung a bare foot back and forth through the water. "Yes, ma'am," he said. "Mind if I come in? It's so warm out here, and I'm all sweaty." He adopted a pose that he called 'The Young Yachtsman,' which involved pulling on an imaginary rope. "I've never been in the presence of a queen before. It's. . . thrilling."

But instead of blushing, Marie laughed – softly at first, then building to full snorts. "Are you trying to flatter me? You, a scrawny boy? Am I on a television prank show?"

"Hey!" Ty said. "I'm not scrawny!"

This only made Marie laugh all the more. She grabbed her sides and rolled about in the fountain, not touching the water at all.

Sage splashed in, too. "We need you to blush!" he said. "We're in a baking competition, and we need – well, it's a long story. But we need to capture your blush."

Marie Antoinette stopped laughing and looked serious for a moment. "I wish I could help you, young master. But the last time I blushed was in seventeen sixty, on my fifth birthday. Since then I've seen just about everything and done just about everything else. I am – how do you say? – shameless! Nothing will make me blush!"

"Oh yeah?" Sage said. He climbed on to the ledge of the fountain. With his chest held high, he cupped one wet hand and slipped it into his armpit. Solemnly, he lifted his elbow up in the air before slamming it back towards his chest.

It was so loud and disturbing a sound that it sent a flock of pigeons squawking up in the air.

But Marie Antoinette only moved her shoulders back and forth, which was as close as she could come to shaking her severed head. "Sorry," she said. "I've farted before major heads of state. It doesn't even make me *laugh* any more."

Ty and Sage both looked to Rose, but she was plumb out of ideas.

Just then they heard an angry howl coming from behind them on the garden path. Suddenly the transparent form of Ourson hurtled into the clearing, sailed over the ledge of the fountain, and fastened his hands around what was left of Marie Antoinette's neck. "How could you say 'Let them eat cake'?" he roared.

"We were starving! All seven of my sisters died while *you* were hosting wine-and-cheese receptions!"

The ghost of Marie's severed head slid from her shoulders and slipped softly into the water.

"Ourson!" Rose scolded.

Shamefacedly, the ghost stepped away from headless Marie Antoinette. "I did not mean to do that!" he said. "I didn't know it would fall off!"

Rose pointed. "Find her head and put it back!"

The ghost looked thoughtful as he sank into the water and swished his insubstantial hands around. "It is *very* slimy, this fountain!" he said. "Why do they not clean it?"

Rose put her hands on her hips. "Just do as you're told."

"Ah-ha!" He rose up out of the water, and in his arms was the startled-looking head of the dead queen. Ourson held it out to her body and placed it in her hands; then she set it in place, but backward.

"I really should find some way of fastening it permanently," she said as she twisted it around the right way.

Rose squinted at the ghost and gasped. There could be no mistake. The ghost's cheeks were very faintly red.

"Sage!" she cried. "Ty!"

Sage grabbed a handkerchief from his pocket, stumbled through the water to the ghost's side, and gently blotted at Marie's cheek. Ty was right behind him with a blue mason jar. Sage turned and dropped the hankie in, and Ty sealed the jar shut.

Marie Antoinette seemed not to have noticed. She was staring at Ourson. "I never thought about it!" she said to him. "All those parties. . . I thought *everyone* was having parties. I'm so sorry for your sisters. . . you handsome, brutish, devastatingly handsome young man!"

Ourson lowered his hands and stepped back. "And I am sorry I beheaded you. *Again.* I suppose you didn't deserve to have your head cut off. In a way, you were merely an accomplice." He bowed. "An exceptionally beautiful accomplice, I might add."

Suddenly there was a shriek from the other side of the fountain. Just across the pool, peering at them through the harsh sun and pointing, was a portly, moustachioed guard.

Rose turned back towards Ourson and Marie Antoinette, but they had disappeared into the water.

"That water is terribly dirty!" the man shouted. "Get out!"

Rose realised that the guard wasn't pointing at the ghosts but at her and her brothers. She sloshed to the ledge of the fountain and pulled herself out. "Sorry!" she yelled back. "We were hot."

Rose turned to Sage, who was carrying the mason jar with Marie Antoinette's blush-stained handkerchief inside. "Let's get this to the hotel. Hopefully Balthazar will be finished translating the last recipe. And I need to change my trousers."

Back at the Hôtel de Notre Dame, Rose and Sage knocked on Balthazar's bedroom door and cracked it open about half a metre. Inside, he was hunched over the Booke, consulting various tables and indexes and maps and charts and lunar almanacs.

"We got the queen's blush," she announced proudly. "Do you have the Ravishing Rugelach recipe?"

"You're kidding!" he said. "Whose cheek did you get?"

"Oh. . . just Marie Antoinette's," Sage said proudly.

"I'm impressed," said Balthazar. "Now, as for the Ravishing Rugelach, I finished translating, but we're gonna have to pick a new recipe for the ROLLED category. This one is impossible. Though at least the main ingredient is in Paris."

"Why?"

Balthazar handed Rose the sheet of paper. "Read it and weep."

Rose looked over the recipe:

Ravishing Rugelach,
for Matrimonial Merriment.

It was in 1645 that the baker Jean ValBliss did make a pilgrimage to the Cathédrale Notre Dame de Paris with his fiancée, the ravishing Anais Amembert, whom he intended to wed on the steps of the cathédrale. But when he did arrive, he did find that a plague had overtaken the land. Jean and Anais proceeded with their wedding, and together did bake these rugelach to serve to their guests, whereupon the town was filled, for a single afternoon, with pure Bliss.

Jean and Anais Bliss did cut one staff of BUTTER into a bowl with one fist of WHITE FLOUR, two fists of SUGAR, and one fist of SOURED CREAM. Afterward he did add the ROLLING MIDNIGHT CHIME OF THE NOTRE DAME BOURDON BELL CALLED EMMANUEL.

"We have to collect the midnight chime of the bell at Notre Dame Cathedral?" said Rose. "How hard could that be?"

A snort came from Rose's front pocket. "Fools rush in where angels fear to tread!" warned a tiny voice.

Rose reached in and scooped out Jacques. "I made the mistake of trespassing in Notre Dame at night once, and I shan't do it again."

"Why?" said Rose. "What's so awful in there? Is the night guard mean?"

"There are *several* night guards," said Jacques. "But they're not human. They are gargoyles. Hideous, monstrous, vengeful creatures who rule over the cathedral like it's their own kingdom."

"Well, what else are we supposed to do?" she asked.

"I haven't figured it out yet," Balthazar said, "but I should know by the end of the evening. Your parents already called and said they'd be out all night chasing an inchworm's shout."

"Is that hard to capture?" Sage asked.

Balthazar scowled. "Have you ever tried to rile up an inchworm? They're the most reasonable things in the universe." He looked back down at the sheet of paper. "Let me work while you three get some dinner, and then we'll figure out what recipe we can substitute for this one."

"How long is that going to take?" Rose asked impatiently.

"Not that long, I think!" Balthazar said with a sparkle in his eyes. "You know, I didn't really want to come to Paris, but now that I'm here, with all of you impossibly young people, I feel about a hundred years younger! I mean, have you seen how fast I've been translating these recipes?"

"You mean faster than one every six months?" Gus called in from the living room.

"What was the last thing you translated, cat?" Balthazar shouted back.

"Why do you two fight all the time?" Rose asked.

"Isn't that what best friends do?" Balthazar whispered. "I couldn't live without that cat. We just like to. . . challenge each other."

Rose read the recipe for Ravishing Rugelach once more.

"Why don't we just use this?" Rose asked. "It can't be *that* difficult to get past a couple of gargoyles."

But Balthazar shook his head. "You don't know what you're talking about. Gargoyles? They're like the opposite of inchworms. If there is something *more* vile and unreasonable in the world, I don't want to know what it is."

"They're that bad?" Rose asked.

Jacques shuddered. "The *worst.*"

Chapter 12

ROMANCING THE STONES

WHILE SAGE AND Ty played video games and Leigh snored, Rose paced around the room, sighing heavily and talking to herself.

"It's come down to me and Lily and Wei Wen, and he is like a master architect of baking. If the category is ROLLED, Lily is going to make a Jittering Jelly Roll, according to what Jacques saw. I have to make something incredible enough to get me through to the finals. What is Balthazar doing in there? He said he was feeling sprightly! We need another plan! Fast!"

"Calm down, Rosicita!" said Ty.

"You don't understand the pressure I'm under!" she screamed. "It's my fault that the Booke is gone! And it's up to me to fix it. Me alone. *Me!*"

"With all due respect, Rose," Sage said, "it was all of

our faults that the Booke got lost. *I* gave Lily the key to the fridge. And *Ty* was the one who wanted to break the Booke out in the first place 'cause he wanted to impress Aunt Lily. And if *Mum and Dad* hadn't left, we wouldn't have had a problem. So it's not just your fault."

"But I was the one that trusted her," said Rose. "I was the one who ate up her praise and then almost left you guys to join her on her psycho roller coaster ride of fame."

"You almost left?" said Sage. "What do you mean?"

Rose bit her lip. The whole nine months since Lily had left, Rose hadn't shared what had really happened. She was too ashamed to tell her family that she had actually considered leaving them forever to be on some stupid TV show. "I mean, figuratively. Let's check on Balthazar's progress."

But when Rose looked in on him, Balthazar was hunched over his Sassanian version of the Booke, snoring. He hadn't even begun to translate another recipe.

"Old men have to sleep sometime, I guess. OK, that's it!" Rose said. "I don't care how dangerous it is; we're going to Notre Dame to get that chime!"

"Rose, I don't want to go," said Sage. "The last time I

was on the roof of a Parisian landmark in the middle of the night, I almost didn't come back down. What are the chances that ROLLED will be the category tomorrow? One in a million."

"Actually, it's one in eight," she replied.

"Oh, in that case," said Sage, "I guess we'd better go."

Rose, Ty, Sage, and Leigh set off out of the hotel, with Gus trailing behind. Jacques sat tucked in the pocket of Rose's sweatshirt, and Sage carried an empty blue mason jar.

Rose pulled at the brass handle of the heavy glass door of the hotel and held it open for her brothers and the cat, then shuffled on through, failing to notice that two more people were shuffling on through at the same moment. She found herself wedged in the doorway between two people, who whined and groaned in French. Rose couldn't tell what they were saying, but it didn't sound very friendly.

After a moment of struggle, Rose squeezed through the door and fell to her knees, where she finally got a good look at the two French people: Miriam and Muriel Desjardins, who were wearing matching red dresses and headbands made of silk roses.

Miriam lost her balance and went sailing into Ty, who tried to catch her in his arms but buckled under her weight, leaving both of them landing in a heap on the concrete sidewalk. Muriel spun around and fell butt first towards Sage, who tossed the blue mason jar up in the air in order to free his hands but missed Muriel's shoulders anyway.

Rose saw the jar flying to its death on the hard concrete and slid towards it with outstretched arms so that it landed in the soft palms of her hands. Unfortunately, Gus had gotten caught up underneath her, and he squealed as he wrestled his hind leg free.

"Please!" he shouted. "I am not a toy! I am a living thing!"

Miriam and Muriel both turned towards Gus and watched in terror as he stood on his hind legs and brushed himself off. "The nerve of you people."

The twins Desjardins turned to each other, wide-eyed, and began to scream.

"Oh boy," said Rose. "Here we go."

The twins scrambled to their feet and backed away from the grey cat with the rumpled ears and bad attitude.

"The cat – he. . . spoke!" Miriam wailed.

"*Shhh!*" Ty shouted, hopping to his feet. He clamped his hand over Miriam's mouth and ushered her into an empty alley on the side of the hotel. Rose followed suit, leading a fainting Muriel.

"I knew it!" Miriam hissed. "I knew there was something creepy about you people! You're witches! You have a talking cat! You probably ride on brooms as well! Didn't I tell you, Muriel?"

Muriel could only cry and struggle to break free from Rose's grip.

"We're not witches!" Ty squealed. "We're magicians!"

"You're magicians?" Miriam said, shivering with terror. "What do you mean, magicians?"

"We're kitchen magicians!" Ty said. "We make magic with food. Magical cakes, pies, cookies. . . you know, things you eat. All very harmless. Fascinating, of course, and powerful, but ultimately harmless. We're from a long line of kitchen magicians. The night that you found us on the deck of the Eiffel Tower, for instance, we were collecting unspoiled rainfall, directly from a storm cloud."

"What about the talking cat?" said Muriel, still staring in terror at Gus, who sat on the pavement with his front legs folded across his chest.

"He was given a Chattering Cheddar Biscuit a long time ago, and he's been able to talk ever since," Ty answered.

"This is all too much. I have to sit down," said Miriam, faltering as she lowered herself to the concrete.

"So, you're not evil?" Muriel whispered.

"No, no, no," Ty said, shaking his head. "But we know someone who is. She's our aunt. That's why we're competing in the Gala. She stole our magical cookbook, and we challenged her to a duel; and if we win the Gala, we get the cookbook back, but if we lose, she keeps it forever and she can do whatever evil thing she wants with it."

Muriel's jaw dropped. "Who is your evil aunt?"

"Lily Le Fay," Rose said, practically spitting the name from her mouth.

Miriam gasped from where she sat on the concrete.

"I knew it!" she shrieked. "She is the one who made us lose!"

"What?" Rose shouted. "How did she do that?"

"We made our famous Key Lime Cupcakes for the SOUR category," said Muriel. "We added lime juice that we had squeezed the night before, as usual."

"We have made the cupcakes over three hundred

times," Miriam added. "To us, it is easier than breathing. They are perfection each time."

"But when Jean-Pierre took a bite, he winced," Muriel went on. "We were devastated. We went back and were about to toss out the lime juice when I noticed that it smelled funny. I tasted it. Someone had replaced our fresh-squeezed lime juice with olive juice."

"I peeked over at Lily Le Fay's garbage," said Miriam, "and I saw an empty can of olives. I know it was her."

"If you are trying to beat her," said Muriel, "we want to help. We'll do anything to make sure she goes up in flames."

Ty grinned. "How much do you know about the Cathédrale Notre Dame?"

"We are closed!" proclaimed the guard at the front of Notre Dame Cathedral.

Rose stood on her tiptoes and looked past the woman into the majestic vault of the cathedral. A few people were still milling about inside.

"What about them?" Rose asked, pointing.

"They will be asked to leave in fifteen minutes," the guardwoman said.

"Fifteen minutes is all we need! Please? It's our last night in Paris!" Rose said.

With a huff, the guard stepped aside so that they could enter.

Rose, Leigh, Ty, Miriam, and Muriel filed past. Sage was about to follow when the guard realised Sage was carrying not a baby in his baby sling but a cat.

The guard raised her arm. "No cats!" she bellowed.

"But it's a toy!" Sage protested. He thumped the cat on its crumple-eared head. "Look how stiff his legs are! Look at how fake this fur looks! No real cat would be this ugly."

Obligingly, Gus kept his legs and body stiff and unyielding.

The woman touched the cat's head, then pulled on one of his ears. "I can see it now – these ears are not very realistic, are they?"

"Nope!" Sage chirped. "Fakity-fake fake!"

And then they were past and walking down the side aisle of the cathedral.

"That," Gus whispered, "was wholly uncalled for. Ugly!? Me?"

"*Non*! Not you!" Muriel said, leaning in to Gus and patting him on his head.

"Now let me get this straight," said Miriam. "We are waiting until midnight, then we are going upstairs to the bell tower and collecting the chime of the bell in this jar?"

"Yes," Ty answered. "But apparently there is some sort of gargoyle problem."

"I don't see what could be so bad about some stone statues," said Muriel.

"Ten minutes until closing!" a voice reverberated through the stone vault of the cathedral. "Everyone is to exit in ten minutes!"

"How are we going to get around the guards?" Rose asked.

Miriam put her arm around Rose's shoulder. "Luckily for you, my sister and I know this cathedral *very* well – including all the best hiding places. Come this way."

Half an hour later, the night security guard had completed his tour around the cathedral, and there was the ominous *thunk* of dead bolts being shot home.

"How will we get out when we're done?" Rose asked as she, her brothers, and the girls came out of a confessional.

"One problem at a time, *mi hermana*," Ty said. "First, let's get that bell toll."

Rose tilted her head back to look at the ceiling, but it was so high and the cathedral so dark that the ceiling might as well have been an open sky on a cloudy night. Every movement Rose made – every shuffle, every twitch, every sniffle, every cough – bounced off the massive marble columns in a frightening echo.

"Let's get this over with," Rose said, checking her watch. It was already 10.30pm. Balthazar had said that Purdy and Albert would be out late, but this was pushing it. "Where is this bell? And where are these infamous gargoyles?"

Miriam was nodding. "The gargoyles are on the same level as the bell tower, up high, overlooking Paris. As for the bell—"

Leigh cleared her throat. "It really depends on the particular bell to which you're referring, young Rose," she said. "There are five bells in Notre Dame. Four are located in the North Tower, but the bell you're thinking of – the Bourdon bell called Emmanuel – is located in the South Tower."

Muriel gasped. "How does the tiny genius child know so much?"

"Magical mishap," answered Ty.

"Normally she can't even tie her shoes," Sage added.

Muriel led the way up a vast spiral staircase of white stone. At the top of the stairs was a tiny doorway – apparently the bishops were shorter back when this place was built. Rose had to duck to get through.

On the other side was a stone balcony overlooking the city. Rose might have been frightened if she hadn't found herself atop the Eiffel Tower just the evening before. Compared to that experience, the cathedral tower felt like it was hugging the ground.

"The bell is through there," said Miriam, pointing to another tiny entryway at the end of the balcony.

"What now?" Sage asked, setting Gus on the ground.

Rose checked her watch: 11.50 pm. "We wait, and at midnight we capture the chime."

"Is that so?" said a low, growling voice.

"Sage?" Ty asked. "Was that you doing a weird gargoyle voice?"

"No!" Sage said, trembling.

In the darkness beside them, something moved. Rose jumped, then turned to discover that the deep shadows at the rear of the balcony had been hiding a gargoyle.

The statue was perched on a pedestal set against the wall; it had a monkey-like face with a protruding snout and tongue, sharp teeth, sunken eyes, and a horn atop its head. Odd little bumps lined its back, and two wings sprouted from its shoulders.

While Rose was studying the statue, not wanting to believe that it had actually just spoken, it turned its head and looked right at her. "Boo!" it said.

Sage yelped, and Ty practically tripped over Gus as he backed into Muriel and Miriam. The twins were staring, horrified, at the stone statue. A fluffy cat who talks is one thing, but a statue in the shape of a demon is quite another.

"I want to go home," Muriel whispered to her sister.

"Why did we trust the baking magicians?" said Miriam.

"It was your idea!" Muriel whispered.

The family watched as the gargoyle's wings broke free from the sides of its sunken ribcage and its stony grey limbs peeled away from the pedestal. The gargoyle lifted its wings and began to flap them. To Rose's surprise, its wings fluttered quickly and delicately – quite like a dragonfly's. The gargoyle rose off the pedestal and buzzed through the air, landing squarely in front of the entry to the room where the bell was kept.

"Nobody will be capturing any chimes tonight!" the gargoyle thundered. "You are trespassing!"

Sage couldn't seem to tear his eyes away from the gargoyle's jagged ribs, beady eyes, and lolling tongue. "Ew," he said.

"What?" the gargoyle snapped. "What did he just say?"

Ty cleared his throat. "He said. . . 'Hello-ew.' Don't mind my brother; it's just his crazy speech impediment. My parents have tried to get it fixed. *Anyway*. . ."

Ty sauntered over to the gargoyle and stuck his hand out. "Hey. I'm Ty, as in the herb thyme. Put her there, buddy. What's your name, my man?"

The gargoyle scowled. "My name," it said, "is Eve."

Ty winced. "You mean. . . you're a girl?"

"Surprised?" the gargoyle asked.

"Not at all!" Ty bluffed. "I call everyone 'man'! Girls, boys, gargoyle girls, gargoyle boys anyway. . ." Ty's offered the girl gargoyle one of his thousand-watt smiles. "You are, like, the most beautiful gargoyle I, for one, have ever laid eyes on!"

"Your flattery won't work up here," came another stony voice. A second gargoyle, this one just a giant head with a wide, fiery grin and the heavy, flowing eyebrows of a Chinese dragon, bounced up from the corner where it lay and rolled along the balcony railing towards Ty. "I'm Bob, Eve's brother. We know we're grotesque. We're not ashamed."

"Speak for yourself," chirped a third gargoyle in a high-pitched, fairy-ish voice near the ceiling. This one had a catlike face with two long tusks; but instead of two ears, its head culminated at the top in a single, odd bulb shape. She leaped down and said, "I wouldn't mind a little flattery. I'm their sister, Antonia."

Ty smiled, searching for something about Antonia to admire. "I really like your. . . head-bulb thing," he finally managed.

Antonia stifled a giddy giggle. "Thank you," she said. "Many say it's my finest feature."

"Antonia!" shouted Bob, bouncing up in the air and landing on the floor of the balcony with a crack. "We're trying to scare them away, not socialise with them! *Please!*"

Bob swivelled in place and addressed Ty in a fearsome voice. "Why do you trespass on our tower?"

Rose pointed a finger meekly up in the air. "Um, I think I can answer that, uh, Bob. My name is Rose, I'm Ty's sister, and we are a family of bakers. We are competing in an international baking competition against our evil aunt to make her remove her dangerous

Secret Ingredient from the market and regain control of our family's magical cookbook. It would be a huge help if we could capture the sound of your bell's magnificent chime. Will you let us?"

The three gargoyle siblings exchanged glances. Eve rustled her wings. "Your plea is compelling," she judged. "But I'm sorry, no. Our only duty is to guard Emmanuel. We have never failed, and we won't fail now."

Sage winked. "Well, this audience is a tough one! It's like they have hearts of stone!"

The gargoyles eyed him warily.

"Maybe a little humour will smooth over the situation—"

"Sage," Rose said, "I don't really think that's a—"

"Hey, what's a gargoyle's favourite soup? Stone soup. What's a gargoyle's favourite hot beverage? Lava. What's a gargoyle's favourite type of music? Rock. What's an alien gargoyle called? A meteorite. Who visits gargoyles when they dream? The Sandstone Man. What happens when a gargoyle laughs? It cracks up. . ." Sage paused. "That's it. That's all I've got."

The gargoyles were unmoved by Sage's humour. All except Eve, who had covered her mouth with one wing as if hiding a smile.

Eve cleared her throat with a terrible stone-grinding sound, then dropped her wing. She wasn't smiling.

"The young redhead is very funny," she barked. "Nevertheless, you will leave before the tolling of the bell."

Rose's shoulders slumped. "Sorry to bother you," she muttered, turning to go.

"Good idea, Rose," Muriel shouted. "Let's get out of here! I feel like I'm inside a nightmare!"

Just then, a chorus of bells began to chime. "Are those the North Tower bells?" Rose asked.

"Yes," Bob grunted. "They anticipate the chiming of our Emmanuel bell, which you shan't witness, because you're leaving *right now*." Bob bounced up in the air and landed with a *CRACK*, breaking one of the marble tiles on the floor and dislodging one of the posts in the railing. It rolled over the edge of the balcony and tumbled a hundred metres through the air to smash to pieces on the walkway below.

Leigh looked coolly at her siblings. "It would appear that they are quite serious about our leaving."

"No kidding!" said Ty. "Let's get out of here!"

Sage and Gus were huddled together in a corner, whispering. Before Rose could ask them what they were doing, Sage broke from the huddle and walked towards Eve. He knelt on one knee and offered her a hand. "We'll go in a minute, I promise. But first, these chiming bells make me want to dance. Will you do me the honour?"

Eve's stern monkey-face seemed to soften. "I don't know what to say," she said in her deep, stony voice. "No one has ever asked me to dance before."

"Really?" Miriam cried. "We're really asking the monsters to dance? You are the strangest bunch of people I have ever met. Americans are so bizarre."

Eve ignored Miriam as she lifted one of her stony paws and placed it in Sage's outstretched hand. As Sage stood, she stood also, stretching up on her hind legs and placing her other paw on Sage's shoulder. The two began to rock back and forth to the music of the chiming bells, both staring awkwardly into the distance.

Ty quickly got the idea. He turned to little cat-like Antonia and offered his hand. *"Mademoiselle?"* he crooned. "May I?"

"Oh heck, yes!" Antonia leaped into Ty's arms, and the two of them waltzed around the dark balcony, Antonia's wings flapping mightily.

Rose knew what she had to do. She quickly retrieved

their final blue mason jar, then whispered, "Jacques!"

The little mouse poked his head out of the pocket of her sweatshirt. "*Oui?*" he said.

"I'll get the jar in position, and you flip the lid when the chime is done, OK?"

Jacques nodded. Rose looked over at Bob. He was rolling gently in place, entranced by his sisters' dancing. Rose inched behind him to the entryway to the bell room. Watching Bob carefully, she reached back and placed the open mason jar on the wooden deck underneath the bell. Jacques jumped to the ground and scurried over to the jar.

As Rose was standing back up, Bob noticed her. "What are you doing?" he thundered.

"I was just. . . pouting because I have no one to dance with," she said, careful to block the view into the bell room as she walked toward him. "That is. . . unless you'll take pity on me, Bob?"

If it is possible for a stone to blush, Bob did. Rose held out her hands, and Bob, who was just a head after all, bopped up and down in front of Rose, and she bopped up and down with him.

Rose looked past the bobbing orb of stone in front of her at her two brothers, both slow-dancing with stone statues, while Miriam picked up Leigh and rocked back and forth and Muriel twirled around the balcony with Gus in her arms.

After a minute, another bell joined the clanging chorus. Rose glanced surreptitiously past Bob and saw the Emmanuel bell swinging pendulously back and forth.

Underneath the bell, poor Jacques shook with every stentorian chime, but he stood firm, clinging to the side of the blue mason jar. When the rolling chime finally ended, he clamped the lid of the jar closed.

Rose stopped bouncing and started clapping. "Yay! That was fun. Our parents are probably worried sick, so we should get going."

Sage broke free from Eve's stony grip, rubbing the mangled tendons in his crushed hand. "Well, it was nice meeting you!"

Ty bowed courteously to Antonia. "*Enchanté, mademoiselle.*"

Rose quickly grabbed the mason jar and stuffed it, along with Jacques, into the front pocket of her sweatshirt. Sage grabbed the cat, and they all started down the spiral staircase.

"Wait!" cried Bob from the doorway. "How will we get in touch with you?"

"When will you be back?" shouted Eve.

"Um. . . tomorrow!" Ty shouted back.

"Don't go!" Antonia roared. A pair of teeth like scythes sprouted from the roof of her mouth, and she soared through the air towards Ty's head.

"Run!" he shouted, pushing past Rose and Sage and Leigh. He swiftly ushered Muriel and Miriam down the cold, white stone steps of the spiral staircase, while Rose scrambled behind with Sage and Leigh.

Rose, who headed up the rear, turned to find an angry Antonia rushing just inches behind her, baring her newly sprouted fangs. "What sort of friends are you?" she howled as Bob and Eve bounced behind her.

Fortunately, the staircase was narrow, and Antonia's vast stone wings got caught, blocking Bob and Eve like a cave-in at a rock quarry.

As soon as Rose set foot once more on the cathedral floor, she heard a massive creaking overhead as Antonia finally wrenched her elbows free. The three came tumbling down the stairs, just in time for the twins and the Bliss clan to sneak out an emergency exit behind the gift shop.

Rose shut the metal door and leaned against it with her back, panting, as she heard the lock click in place.

"Nooooo!" she heard Bob shout in a muted blast.

"I feel bad," said Sage. "Should we go back in?"

"They're made out of stone, Sage. They'll get over it," said Ty.

Outside, the air was deliciously crisp, more like an autumn night than a spring one, and the lights outside the cathedral glowed a dim orange. Rose took the blue mason jar with the chime out of her pocket and looked at it. They had done it!

"You were. . . quite dashing in there, Thyme," said Muriel, putting a hand on his shoulder.

"A wonderful performance," Miriam agreed.

Ty looked as though he might melt into a hot puddle on the sidewalk.

Just then, Rose noticed someone slinking towards them through the shadows of the courtyard.

He moved into the light. It was Lily's assistant, the Shrunken Man!

He stared at Rose, grinned, then dragged his finger slowly across his neck.

Rose gasped, and her hands went limp.

The blue mason jar shattered on the cold stone walkway, and the midnight chime of the Emmanuel bell rang out into the night, before fading away into nothing.

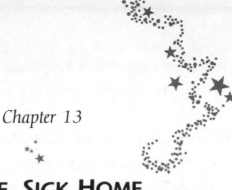

Chapter 13

HOME, SICK HOME

ROSE SLEPT A grand total of about forty-five minutes that night. She rolled back and forth in her bed, replaying the moments before she dropped the jar over and over again.

Maybe there will come a day when I make no more mistakes, Rose thought on waking the next morning. Purdy had once told her that everyone made mistakes, and Rose believed it; but since she really only witnessed her own, it seemed to Rose as if she was a lot clumsier than everyone else.

Rose rifled through the mason jars in Balthazar's suitcase: traditional ingredients like flour and sugar snuggled beside blue mason jars filled with the unspoiled rainfall from the other evening and the handkerchief with Marie Antoinette's blush, plus the newly added murderer's growl and banshee's howl. But no rolling chime. What would they do if the category was ROLLED?

"In a moment," Jean-Pierre proclaimed, "I will announce today's theme. Today's bake-off will determine the final two chefs, who will compete tomorrow in the Wild Card category."

All the kitchens were empty and covered by a dusting of flour except for the three with the final contestants: Rose, Lily, and Wei Wen.

Rose glanced up at the balcony where her family was sitting. Miriam and Muriel were sitting with them, staring down intently at the three remaining kitchens. Rose wasn't sure if they were there because they wanted to see Lily go up in flames or because they wanted to hang around Ty, but it didn't really matter. It was nice to have more people rooting for her.

The whole family was grinning at her, except for Sage, who was frowning and staring off into the distance. Sage was particularly upset at the loss of the chime: for the first time in his life, he had managed to sweep a girl off her feet – a girl made of stone, but a girl nonetheless. His cleverness had saved the day, until his boneheaded older sister un-saved it.

"There are three of you left," Jean-Pierre continued. "Who will survive? And who will leave at the end of the day knowing that the finest achievement of her bitter life was just barely out of her reach?"

Rose let her forehead thump on to the kitchen counter.

"The category of the day is. . ." Rose held her breath. *Don't say* ROLLED, she prayed. *Don't say* ROLLED.

". . .SUGARLESS."

Rose heaved a sigh of relief. The jar full of unspoiled rainfall was still very much intact. In the balcony, Sage and the rest of her family gave her a giant thumbs-up.

As Jean-Pierre waddled offstage, Rose pulled the folded recipe for Better-Than-Anything Banana Bread from the back pocket of her jeans.

Ty leaned over Rose's shoulder and stared down at the paper. "Thanks for letting Miriam and Muriel come along last night," he said, having perked up considerably since the night before. "They totally dig me now. I mean, look at them! They're sitting with Mum and Dad! I'll bet it's because I was vulnerable. Girls love to see a boy get all disappointed."

"*Shhh*," Rose hissed. "I'm trying to memorise this before we have to bake."

Ty hopped up and sat atop the rolling chopping block. "You know, I think you're taking this whole thing a little too seriously, Rose."

Rose spun around and stared at her older brother. "I'm taking it too seriously?" she hollered. "What could be more serious than getting our Cookery Booke back?"

Ty thought earnestly for a moment. "Well, if one of us was sick, I guess. Or missing. Something like that. *That* would be serious. This is only a book, Rose. It doesn't matter as much as any one of us."

"Well, it matters to me," Rose replied. "This is the most serious thing I've ever done. So are you going to help me or not?"

An hour later, Rose prepared a bowl of dry ingredients while Ty mashed bananas. "I think we're gonna blow Lily out of the water!" he cried as he pounded at the yellow fruit.

Across the aisle, Lily was working on a Soprano's Wedding Cake that had a layer of sponge, a layer of white chocolate mousse, a layer of blackberry compote, a layer of hazelnut nougatine, and several other delicious-looking layers that Rose couldn't even hope to identify. All of it was tucked neatly under a white chocolate dome, infused with the soaring lilt of a Scandinavian soprano and a dash of Lily's Magic Ingredient. It was an architectural miracle, and probably a culinary one as well, to say nothing of its magical properties.

Rose looked down at her own entry, which at the moment consisted entirely of a bowl of mushed bananas.

"This looks like garbage," Rose said.

"Maybe," Ty agreed. "But I look great. That ought to count for something, right?"

Rose rolled her eyes as she dumped flour, egg, and vanilla with the banana mash. After she stirred it all together, she poured in a half cup of the unspoiled rainfall. Instantly, the batter lost the unappealing, greyish colour of baby food and took on a radiant, golden glow. Rose dipped a spoon into the batter and tried it.

The SUGARLESS batter was the sweetest thing she'd ever tasted – not the cloying, chemical sweetness of aspartame and candy and diet soda, but a natural, delicious sweetness with more flavour than even maple syrup or honey.

Oh my, Rose thought. *Maybe we might even. . . win?*

Twenty minutes later, Rose took the freshly baked

bread out of the oven and plated a slice of her golden banana bread on a simple white dish just before the *ding* of the giant wall timer.

Across the aisle, Lily had plated her intricate dome of cake next to the white-chocolate sculpture of a dove. When Lily sliced through the centre of her cake, Rose could see that the differently coloured layers of cake were arranged to paint a picture: a scene of doves and unicorns frolicking gaily through a meadow.

Wei Wen adjusted his glasses and stood proudly next to his creation. He had fashioned a chocolate replica of Notre Dame that stood five feet high and seven feet across.

Rose looked down at her modest slice of banana bread. *Then again,* she thought, *maybe we* won't *win.*

Marco whisked Lily's Soprano's Wedding Cake and Rose's Better-Than-Anything Banana Bread towards Jean-Pierre's table with ease, but he had a harder time with Wei Wen's chocolate Notre Dame. He inched along the black-and-white aisle, the audience gasping with every microscopic tilt of the chocolate sculpture. When finally Marco set the cathedral down in front of Jean-Pierre, everyone breathed a collective sigh of relief, save for Rose.

Jean-Pierre tasted Lily's Soprano's Wedding Cake first. "*Mon Dieu!*" he gasped, peering with wonder at the cross section of the cake. "A scene of doves and unicorns created out of sponge and mousse! I've never seen anything like it!"

Jean-Pierre cut through the scene with his fork and tasted it. "It's. . ." he trailed off. "It's. . ."

As Rose watched, the master chef's eyes dulled, and his voice became slightly robotic. "How very sweet," he said. "However did you manage this without sugar, Lily dear. You are the sovereign of sweetness."

The cameras followed Jean-Pierre as he turned his attention to the chocolate replica of Notre Dame. The master chef fell to his knees and began to weep. "It is perfection!" he cried. "Why, why did I never think to attempt a chocolate cathedral?"

The great chef climbed to his feet and took a forkful of the South Tower, where just eleven hours ago, Rose and her brothers had been dancing with gargoyles. Jean-Pierre closed his eyes and savoured the bite. "Sensational," he whispered, tears streaming down his cheeks.

I'm toast, Rose thought.

Finally, the cameras followed Jean-Pierre down the

table to Rose's plate. The master chef looked at her slice of banana bread and furrowed his brow.

"*Mademoiselle*, forgive me; I am confused," he said. "Where is the baked good?"

Rose pointed sheepishly to the slice of golden bread. "That's it."

"But what does it do?" Jean-Pierre said, poking the slice with a fork. "Does it sing? Does it speak five languages? Does it bake more impressive baked goods?"

Rose shook her head as Jean-Pierre reluctantly took a bite of the banana bread. He closed his eyes, swallowed, and walked to his microphone without saying a word.

Ty patted Rose on the back. "I guess we should have made the Golden Gate Bridge out of pralines or something," he said.

Jean-Pierre tapped the microphone. "The decision was difficult in one respect, and simple in another. Choosing the winner was simple. Choosing who to eliminate was nearly impossible."

Rose hung her head. At least it hadn't been *easy* for Jean-Pierre to send her home.

"First, I will share the contestant who is safe, and who will move on to tomorrow's final showdown. Coming in second place today is. . ."

Rose crossed her fingers.

". . .Lily Le Fay."

The audience erupted in applause as Lily forced herself to smile and wave.

"Now, the simple decision. The winner of today's SUGARLESS challenge is. . . Rosemary Bliss!"

The crowd let out an audible gasp. Rose's knees went weak, and she sagged against the side of the stage.

"I know it seems strange," the master chef was saying, "but with a simple slice of banana bread, this young baker has shattered the lofty dreams of the chocolate Notre Dame. Its architect, Wei Wen, may now exit the expo centre."

Wei Wen fell to the floor, sobbing, as the South Tower of his chocolate Notre Dame crumbled to the ground.

"And then there were two," Jean-Pierre continued. "Tomorrow will be, undoubtedly, the most important day of their lives."

You have no idea, Rose thought. Jean-Pierre was under the impression that only Rose's reputation was at stake. He didn't know that her family's most precious heirloom and the happiness of her beloved town were on the line as well.

Lily stepped to Rose's side in front of the stage.

"Congratulations," Lily said through gritted teeth. Glancing around to make sure the microphones weren't close enough to pick up her words, she leaned in to Rose's ear. "I'm going to *crush* you tomorrow." Lily looked like a movie star and smelled like a queen, but she sounded like a murderer.

Rose felt icy fingers of fear trickle down her back at her aunt's threat. Jerking away, Rose saw pure anger in her aunt's eyes, but also, behind the anger. . . maybe a hint of fear? After all, Rose's simple banana bread had defeated her aunt's spectacular cake, complete with its magical ingredient *and* Lily's Magic Ingredient.

And that's when Rose knew – while Rose was competing for the Booke and to stop Lily's Magic Ingredient, the only thing Lily cared about was winning.

And that gave Rose an idea. Maybe she and Lily could both get what they wanted. Rose had won the day, after all – maybe now she had a little leverage. Rose leaned in to give Lily a kiss on the cheek, and while she was there she whispered, "I'll let you win tomorrow if you promise to stop selling the Magic Ingredient and return the Booke."

Lily laughed. "Now I understand why you chickened out right before you were supposed to come to New

York with me, Rose," she said. She gripped Rose's hand a little more tightly. "You don't have what it takes to make it on such a big stage. You don't have the guts."

Rose considered for a moment. "I'm pretty scared, it's true. There's a lot on the line. But at least I'm brave enough to compete without using secret chemicals in my baking to make people like me."

Lily looked like she wanted to slap Rose across the cheek. With the cameras watching, Lily gave her a kiss instead. "Let's both do what we do best and see who comes out on top in the end, shall we?" she whispered.

At the hotel that night, Albert made his famous Family Fajitas. He set out plates of sour cream, peppers and onions, tortillas, guacamole, black beans, and grilled steak; and everyone – including dinner guests Miriam and Muriel – went around the table assembling their own fajitas. Everyone, that is, except for Jacques, who nibbled on a piece of Monterey Jack as big as himself; Gus, who dozed in a tight knot of fur on the ottoman; and Leigh, who turned her nose up at the whole smorgasbord, which was odd considering that Family Fajitas were usually Leigh's favourite meal.

But not since eating Lily's Magic Ingredient. "I'll not

eat steak rolled up like a hot dog, thank you very much," she said snootily.

"Then maybe you'll eat this instead," said Purdy, stepping out of the kitchen with a slice of cake on a plate. "Open up!" she commanded.

Leigh rolled her eyes at her mother but dutifully opened her mouth as Purdy slid in the slice of cake.

"That ought to do it," Purdy said. "It's a Matching Muffin! I calibrated it to who Leigh truly is so that she'll match who she was before she ate Lily's Magic Ingredient. It's no Turn-Back Trifle, but it should do the trick."

Leigh burped daintily, then said, "It's a Matching Muffin!" in Purdy's voice. She snorted and said it again.

Rose and Ty looked at each other, bewildered. It was the strangest thing Rose had ever seen – or heard. It was as if her mother's voice had jumped into Leigh's mouth.

"That's not how it was supposed to work," Purdy said.

"Incredible!" Miriam gasped.

"Incredible!" Leigh mimicked back.

Albert ran his hands through his hair. "Oh, perfect."

"Oh, perfect!" Leigh repeated with Albert's deep voice. Then she burst out laughing.

"That's quite enough, young lady!" Albert said. "We'll deal with this new talent of yours later. But first—" He held up his water glass in a toast. "To Rose and Ty, for their victory today. I think you're both ready for the Wild Card category tomorrow."

Rose sighed heavily as she gnawed on a piece of spicy steak. She'd been ignoring the eventuality of the dreaded Wild Card, but it had, at last, arrived.

"How are we going to do it?" she asked.

Purdy wiped steak juice from the corner of her mouth. "Whatever the category is, we'll just pick a recipe accordingly, and hope that Balthazar can translate it in an hour!"

Balthazar barely looked up from his fajita, which had collapsed on to his plate in a mess of sour cream and onions.

"But what if the recipe requires an ingredient we don't have?" Rose went on, pushing her plate to the centre of the table. "What if it's something we can't get in Paris, in an hour?"

Rose burst up from her seat and paced around the

coffee table in the living room while the rest of her family continued to eat their fajitas.

"Just let her pace around," Rose heard Ty murmur. "I think she'll tire herself out."

It was there, on the coffee table, that Rose spotted a large manila envelope with her name on it. "What's this?" she asked, waving the envelope in the air.

Albert tried to speak through a mouthful of refried beans. "The bellhop brought it earlier," he said.

Rose tore open the thick manila envelope and found an unmarked DVD inside. *Great,* she thought. *It's probably some threat from Lily's assistant.*

Rose popped the DVD into the suite's player. Instead of the glimmering green eyes and bushy black brows of the Shrunken Man, Rose saw the sweeping blond bangs of Devin Stetson. Her stomach jumped around inside of her like a captive frog in a jar.

"Hi, Rose," he said, staring straight out from the screen. He sighed listlessly, but the corners of his mouth were turned upward into a smile. "We here at Stetson's Doughnuts and Automotive Repair wanted to wish you good luck at the Gala des. . ." Devin trailed off and yelled to the man in overalls standing behind him. "What is it, Dad? Oh, right. Gala des Gâteaux Grands.

You guys are amazing bakers, the best in the whole world, and we know you'll win. But don't take my word for it!"

The camera panned through the aisles of Borzini's Nuttery and settled on the peanut-shaped figure of Mr Borzini himself, who hoisted a burlap sack of sunflower seeds atop a tall stack of burlap sacks, then wiped his hands on his apron and laughed into the camera.

"What's going on here?"

"We're making a movie for Rose Bliss," Devin said from behind the camera. "She's competing in that French contest."

"Oh, sure," said Mr Borzini, waving into the camera. "Hi, Rose. Hello, Purdy, Albert, kids. You'll be great, Rose."

The camera panned down the main street of Calamity Falls and stopped inside Florence's Flowers, where Florence had fallen asleep in her chair.

Devin's hand wandered into the frame and tugged at Florence's sleeve. She awoke with a start. "What? What's this contraption for? Why are you taking my picture?"

"It's a video camera, Florence. I'm making a video for the Blisses, to tell them good luck at the Gala des Whatever."

"Oh," said Florence, staring through her Coke bottle glasses. "I just hope they come back in one piece. Calamity Falls would be lost without 'em."

Rose winced. She knew that Calamity Falls was already lost, and would be lost forever if she didn't win the Wild Card battle the next day.

By then the Blisses had finished their fajitas and had gathered on the couches behind Rose to watch the DVD.

The camera panned over the outdoor café tables at Pierre Guillaume's French bistro. Pierre Guillaume himself stood in the entrance to the café, wrists tucked limply into the pockets of his chef's coat.

"I wish to wish the family Bliss the very best of luck in my beloved hometown of Paris." He sighed. "I am very excited for them."

"He doesn't sound excited," said Sage. "He sounds like he just found out he needs a root canal."

"There's no one at the café," Ty remarked. "Jeez, where is everybody?"

The camera panned over to the only people sitting at the cast-iron tables: Mr Bastable and Mrs Thistle-Bastable. They were sipping spoonfuls of French onion soup, staring into the distance.

Mr Bastable looked directly into the camera. "I miss the Blisses. They make wonderful muffins, but mostly, they're just nice people." Then he turned back to his soup. Mrs Thistle-Bastable smiled wanly.

"This is so sweet of everybody," said Purdy, pulling Rose on to her lap. "See, Rose? It doesn't matter if you win tomorrow. Everyone in town still loves us."

"But look at them!" Rose yelled. "The whole town is grey. And it's my fault. I have to fix it."

Rose shot off of Purdy's lap and ran into her room, slamming the door behind her.

Later that night, after the Desjardins twins had returned to their room and everyone else had gone to sleep, Rose found herself tossing and turning in bed, praying that the Booke would magically fall through the ceiling and land next to her on her pillow. She would cradle it in her arms, and if she went out, she would carry it in a baby sling so it would never again stray from her sight.

While Leigh snored in the bed next to hers, Rose looked over the walls of her hotel bedroom. There were framed prints of old French advertisements from the 1900s for bars of soap and hats and corsets. There was a bookshelf with a few thick books stacked on top, one of which was just about the same size and colour as the Cookery Booke itself.

Rose got out of bed and crossed to the bookshelf. She slid the heavy book down from the shelf and blew a half inch of dust off the top. She opened the book, praying that somehow, through some bit of magic, it might be the Cookery Booke.

"What fools these mortals be...," she read. Of course. The collected works of William Shakespeare.

Rose sighed. The book could have fooled her. It could have fooled anyone.

It could have fooled anyone.

Rose gasped. She ran across the suite into Sage and Ty's room and jumped on Sage's bed.

"Ty! Sage! Wake up!"

Ty threw a pillow at Rose's head, and Sage buried himself deeper into his blankets.

"Look what I found in my room!" Rose held up the Booke look-alike.

"The Cookery Booke!" Sage said.

"No, it's a book of Shakespeare plays. But it *looks* like the Booke! If we can get Lily out of her room, we can steal the Booke back and leave this as a decoy!"

Sage groaned. "Rose, the last time we were up there, we couldn't even *find* the Booke. And what's the point of leaving a decoy anyway? As soon as they open it, they'll see that it's not the Booke."

"But maybe they won't open it right away!" Rose replied. "If they win the competition, then get on the plane carrying the book, open it up on the plane, and realise it's not the Booke, by then it'll be too late! Imagine the look on her smug, stupid face."

"But Rose," Ty said, his hair sticking out at ridiculous angles. "How are we supposed to get Lily out of her room? It's the middle of the night, remember?"

Leigh wandered in. "How are we supposed to get Lily out of her room?" she said, mimicking Ty's voice exactly.

Rose smiled at her brothers. "That's the best part of my idea," she said. "Leigh, how would you like to talk to Lily, the magnificent mistress of muffins, on the phone?"

Chapter 14

A (TINY) THIEF IN THE NIGHT

"Hello, I would like to speak with Ms Lily Le Fay, *s'il vous plaît.*"

"And who may I say is calling?"

"Monsieur Jean-Pierre Jeanpierre," said Leigh with Jean-Pierre's haughty, robust French accent.

"But, sir, it is 4am."

Rose sat beside Leigh while she spoke on the phone with the front-desk manager. Rose told her what to say, and a moment later, Leigh repeated it in the voice of the pompous French chef. It was uncanny.

"I think she will want to accept this phone call," said Leigh in Jean-Pierre's voice. "I am calling to discuss her victory at the Gala des Gâteaux Grands this morning."

"Right away!" said the clerk. The phone rang again,

and Leigh held up the receiver as Lily answered.

"What?" Lily asked groggily, her voice ringing out from the receiver.

"Lily," said Leigh. "It is Jean-Pierre. We would like to plan a publicity event in regards to your victory. Something the entire world will see."

Lily was silent a moment. "Are you saying I've already won?"

"I can't imagine any other possible outcome," said Leigh.

"What did you have in mind for this publicity event?"

"I can't discuss it over the phone," said Leigh. "You'll have to meet me in my office at the expo centre."

"Now?"

"There is no time like the present! True confectioners never sleep!"

Lily said, "But can't this wait a few more hours? It's barely four in the morning."

Leigh looked to Rose, who shrugged. Frustrated, Leigh spoke in her normal voice. "It's only just across the street, lazybones!"

Silence stretched down the phone line. At last Lily asked, "Why did you just sound like a little girl?"

Leigh cleared her throat. "I suffer from stomach pains,"

she said in Jean-Pierre's voice again. "It is terrible. Now, will you come?"

"Give me ten minutes," Lily said.

Leigh hung up, and Rose, Ty, and Sage went to peer out the window, which overlooked the sidewalk in front of the Hôtel de Notre Dame.

Twelve minutes later, they saw Lily and the Shrunken Man hurrying across the street to the expo centre.

"Now's our chance!" Rose said.

Moments later, Rose, Ty, Sage, and Leigh, with Sage carrying Gus in the baby sling and Jacques nestled in Rose's sweatshirt pocket, skidded to a halt in front of the secret elevator. Standing before it, vacuuming the carpet, was a maid in a conservative black frock.

The maid shut off the vacuum when she saw them. "This area is restricted, young woman," she said. She looked down at Gus. "Particularly for cats."

Leigh held up the key they'd been given last time they'd visited Lily's suite. "But we have the key!" she said.

The maid shook her head. "You must be mistaken," she said. "There are only two people staying on the Fantasy Floor, and I know both of them. Now shoo!"

As they retreated back across the lobby, Ty muttered, "Now what?"

Rose glanced at a house phone on the other side of the hotel lobby. "Leigh, can you do Lily's voice?"

Leigh grinned devilishly. "Of course, darling," she said in Lily's sugary sweet tone.

On the lobby phone was a button that automatically rang the front desk. Rose pressed the button and held the phone up to Leigh.

The kids watched as the clerk picked up the ringing telephone. "Good morning, this is the Hôtel de Notre Dame front desk," he said. "How may I help you?"

"Hello, it is Lily Le Fay," Leigh said quietly. "I've spilled water on my kitchen counter. I need a maid to come and mop it up. Immediately."

"Of course, Ms Le Fay!" said the clerk in a panic. "Do not lift a finger! We will be right there!"

The clerk hung up and jogged over to the maid. "There's an emergency on the Fantasy Floor!" he cried. "Lily Le Fay has spilled water on her kitchen counter! Go!"

The maid promptly shut off her vacuum and hurried into the elevator. Rose waited until the elevator departed. Then she looked at her siblings. "Our turn," she said.

Ty nodded. "But we'd better hurry. It won't take Lily long to figure out she's been tricked."

Moments later, they arrived in the Fantasy Floor antechamber. The door to Lily's suite was already open. Rose peered in and saw the maid wiping up the nonexistent water spill on the kitchen counter. While she was occupied, the kids slipped through the door and hid in the bathroom until the maid left.

They split up to search the suite. Rose and Ty checked Lily's bedroom, but all they found were a closet full of black cocktail dresses, twelve identical cotton bathrobes, hundreds of bottles of high-end skin care products, two dozen boxes of high-heeled sandals, and a shelf of self-help books with titles like *Don't Ask for What You Want – Take It!*

Rose peeked under each of the shoe boxes, in between every dress, behind every self-help book, but the Bliss Cookery Booke was nowhere to be found.

Sage, who ransacked the kitchen, and Leigh, who crawled through the master bathroom, had similar luck.

They met back in the main room of the suite. Sage looked perplexed. "Lily must have locked our Booke in a Swiss bank," he said. "Where the heck could she be hiding it?"

Gus and Jacques were perched on the windowsill, watching for the inevitable return of Lily and the Shrunken Man. "I am sure I don't know," said the stodgy cat, "but now may not be the best time to discuss it. Lily and her assistant just left the expo centre, and they don't look happy."

Sage picked up Gus and fastened him back into the baby sling. As Rose reached for Jacques, he held up a single paw. "I will stay," he announced. "I will spy all night and discover the location of your prized book."

"You can't!" said Ty, playing lookout from the door of the suite. "It's too dangerous!"

"There is no choice," Jacques said. "If there is foul play tomorrow and Rose does not emerge victorious, you must know where the book is so that you can retrieve it."

Rose was stunned. So, apparently, was Gus. "Jacques," the cat said, hanging from Sage's chest in the baby sling. "I never thought I would be saying this to a mouse, but your nobility of character rivals that of a Scottish Fold. You are a cat among mice."

Jacques bowed to the cat, saluted the kids, and, with a cry of *"Vive la France!"* darted to the floor and through a hole in the baseboard.

"That was really touching," said Ty, "but any moment now Lily's creepy little boyfriend is going to run in here and shoot us in the neck with a poison dart gun or something. Can we go already?"

Leigh nodded. "Can we go already?" she repeated in Ty's voice.

Rose and her siblings piled into the secret elevator and rode it back down to the lobby. They were just in time. As they waited for the regular elevator to take them to their own suite, they saw Lily rushing across the lobby on her way back in.

She was by herself.

"Hey, guys," Rose said. "Not that I really want to see him, but where is the Shrunken Man?"

Sage shrugged. "Who cares?"

"Yeah," agreed Ty. "It really doesn't matter."

"Why not?" asked Rose.

"'Cause we're totally gonna win tomorrow," he said. "It's not even a question. Whatever theme pops up, we have the ingredients to cover it. We got so much crazy stuff this week."

Rose smiled. "Yeah," she said, shaking her head at the big, fat book she'd wanted to leave in place of the real Booke. It hadn't been much of a plan: Lily would have known it wasn't the Cookery Booke right away. "We really did."

When they got back to their suite, Rose pulled out her room key only to discover that the front door was already ajar.

"Guys," she whispered. "Did we leave the door open?"

Ty and Sage looked at each other, then they looked at Leigh. She just shrugged.

Rose pushed the door open and flicked on the light.

Standing in the centre of the living room, sneering at them, was the Shrunken Man. He held a suitcase in one hand – Balthazar's suitcase, the one that contained all of their magical ingredients!

The Shrunken Man sketched a little bow. "Hello, children," he croaked in a voice like sandpaper. "That was a clever trick, luring us away from our suite. Did you think that when Lily and Jeremius got to Jean-Pierre's office—"

"Who is Jeremius?" Ty huffed.

"Me! As I was saying, did you think that when Lily and Jeremius found Jean-Pierre's office empty, we wouldn't figure out what you had done?" Jeremius lifted the suitcase, his eyes glittering green.

Ty stepped forward. Rose had never seen him looking

so serious. "There's nothing you want in that suitcase, *hombre*," he said softly. "So I suggest you put it down."

Jeremius laughed. "I *laugh*!" he said. "Ha-ha!" He set down Balthazar's suitcase, then opened it so they could see what they knew was inside: It was filled with blue mason jars. The ghostly gust, the true queen's blush, the secret of the *Mona Lisa*'s smile, and all of the other specialty ingredients that Rose and her family had spent the past week so painstakingly collecting. "When we were inside the expo centre and figured out we'd been duped, we decided to loot *your* ingredients. To teach you a lesson in playing fair!"

Without thinking, Rose lunged across the room. Quick as a wink, Jeremius snapped the suitcase shut and leaped on to the back of a couch.

"I don't think so," he croaked.

Sage was fuming. "Who *are* you?" he asked. "What group home for homicidal dwarves did Lily rescue you from?"

"Oh, I'm one of the family," crowed Jeremius. "So I'm sure you won't mind if I borrow these for a little while?"

"Actually, we do!" Ty cried. He and Sage sprang at Jeremius from opposite ends of the couch, while Rose dived straight at him.

But they were too slow.

With a deft acrobatic flip, he somersaulted out the window, the suitcase clutched to his chest, landing astride the wide window ledge. "Ha-ha!" He blew them a wet kiss, then ran away along the ledge, leaping on to a nearby rooftop and prancing along its peak. They watched him caper and listened to his fading cackles as he became a silhouette in the pink-hued light of dawn.

Rose hung her head. "That's it," she sobbed. "We might as well go home."

Chapter 15

AN UNUSUAL CHALLENGE

THAT MORNING, ROSE walked into the expo centre to find everything rearranged. All of the dusty kitchens had been cleared away, leaving the vast room empty save for two kitchens that stood face-to-face: hers and Lily's.

The balconies lining the sides of the room were overflowing with curious audience members, but no one stood on the actual floor of the centre except for Rose and Ty, Lily and Jeremius, and about twenty-five men and women with cameras and microphones on poles and endless coils of brightly coloured wire.

Across the aisle, Lily was wearing her signature black cocktail dress. Her fake black hair tumbled in perfect curls like a cartoon princess's.

Rose could see her own reflection in one of the shiny pots on Lily's stovetop: her thin black hair was dirty and stringy, and she'd pulled it back into a messy ponytail. She looked like she hadn't slept in days. And her green hoodie was covered with flecks of dried batter on the chest and sleeves that smelled like stale eggs and chocolate.

But Rose wasn't worried about how she looked at that particular moment. She was worried about what she had to work with in the competition, which was nothing.

Rose leaned against the counter, dizzy with despair. Last night's mission to recover the Booke had been a terrible mess, and it had ruined her – all because she didn't trust herself to be able to win in the Wild Card category. Now she was sure she would lose. Jeremius had run off with all of their special ingredients. There was no way an ordinary baked good could beat one of Lily's magical ones, especially if they were infused with the Magic Ingredient.

Lily waved to Rose, then held up a small wire birdcage. In a corner of the cage shivered a tiny grey mouse curled up in a ball.

"Jacques!" Rose cried.

"Oh, is that his name?" Lily said. "Clever, to arrange for a mouse as a spy. But alas, he has a weakness for

Camembert. I put a chunk in this decorative birdcage, and he could not resist."

Lily set the cage atop her pantry shelf of ingredients and wiped her hands on her skirt. "Filthy," she muttered.

Just then, the vast chandeliers that hung from the ceiling of the expo centre went dark. An ominous drumroll filled the room, and then the lights burst on, revealing the rotund master of baking at the microphone.

"This is the final countdown!" he bellowed. "Two contestants remain: Lily Le Fay, celebrity chef extraordinaire, and Rosemary Bliss, child." The applause was deafening.

Rose couldn't help looking across the aisle at Lily's kitchen. Throughout her career, Lily had done every low-down, sneaky, cheating thing she could to stomp out anyone who'd gotten in her way. And now she was about to stomp out Rose.

Jean-Pierre exhaled a shaky breath into the microphone. "I would like to say a word now about Lily Le Fay." He paused a minute to wipe the corner of his eye. "I will do my best to contain my tears, but I promise nothing."

A white screen the size of the entire gymnasium wall at Calamity Falls Middle School descended from the ceiling, and a Celine Dion song began to play in the background. Images of Lily's performance over the past four days began appearing on the screen, each 'candid' photograph more polished and perfect than the last.

"Lily Le Fay is simply a master," Jean-Pierre said. "Her baked goods are like professionally wrapped presents: glossy, colourful, and filled with wondrous surprises. And Lily herself is like a present as well. Between her television show and her cookbooks, her patented whisks and bowls and spatulas and beaters, Lily has conquered the world of celebrity baking. It seems there is no stopping her."

The crowd erupted into a tsunami of applause. The slide show ended with a picture of a smiling Lily licking a dollop of whipped cream off her finger.

Can we just get to the announcement of the category, already? Rose thought, tapping her foot on one of the tiles of the kitchen floor.

"And then there is, of course, the young Miss Bliss." Jean-Pierre's tears ceased as he scratched the coarse bristles under his nose. "In her time here, Miss Bliss has created a blackened cookie, an orange ball, an angel food cake, and a banana bread. She's been assisted by her very attractive older brother, Thyme, who has spent much of the competition smiling into the cameras. Today she seems not to have combed her hair or to have changed her sweatshirt, which is not so surprising given that she is a middle school student."

That's it, Rose thought, starting to untie her apron. *I'm outta here.*

"I never suspected that young Rosemary would survive even the first day of competition," Jean-Pierre continued. "And indeed, her blackened cookie was a close call. But then imagine my surprise when I tasted her orange ball, her angel food cake, and her banana bread, and found that I had never in my life been so delighted, so charmed, so. . . moved. . . by a simple baked good."

Rose stopped fumbling with her apron strings as her stomach jumped into her throat. *Jean-Pierre Jeanpierre, the world's foremost judge of baked goods, has never been more delighted than when he was eating my banana bread?*

"I have watched Rosemary at her work throughout the week. Not only do her focus, poise, and technical skill rival that of seasoned professionals, but she bakes with a certain level of. . . we might call it grace. Humble grace."

Humble grace? Rose thought, dumbstruck.

The master chef continued. "I recognise a quality in her that only one other person possesses, and that person is myself: It is the quality of having been born to bake."

Rose gulped. *Maybe I could win*, she thought. *Maybe it isn't all about who has the best ingredients and the most magical help and all that. Maybe it's about who is the most passionate about baking, and helping people feel better.*

Then again, maybe passion just wasn't enough.

"And now for the surprise theme of the day," Jean-Pierre said.

Here it comes.

Whatever the theme would be – whether it was FLAKY or DOUGHY or RAW or BURNED or RANCID or whatever bizarre thing Jean-Pierre had dreamed up in his angel food cake–assisted sleep – Rose would be utterly unable to execute a dish that could stack up against Lily's. She had nothing magical at her disposal, not even a girlish giggle or the first wind of autumn. The Dwarf of Perpetual Sleep was asleep elsewhere, and the true queen's blush had disappeared into the night.

"The theme is UNUSUAL GRAINS."

The room erupted into whispers and gasps as the

audience in the balconies expressed their surprise.

"You'll have one hour to gather and plan, as usual, and then the most important hour of baking in your lives will commence. Go now. Venture forth into your imaginations."

The bald chef left the stage as the balconies began to clear. Rose leaned back against the counter. What was she going to do?

"Oh man, *mi hermana*," Ty said. "You don't look so good. You need to wash your face. Your eyes are all wet."

Rose went to wipe her cheek with the sleeve of her hoodie, but at just that moment Balthazar appeared and yanked her arm away. "Leave it!" he cried.

Balthazar set down the brocade carpet bag he'd been carrying and pried it open.

"Grandpa Balthazar," Rose pleaded, "what am I supposed to do? Jeremius took all of our magical ingredients!"

Balthazar pulled a test tube from the carpet bag and held it underneath Rose's eyelids, which were spilling over like the top tier of a fountain. A few of the tears pooled at the bottom of the test tube. Balthazar stuck a cork in it and handed it to Ty.

"What's this for?" Ty asked, gingerly pinching the vial of tears between the tips of his thumb and forefinger like it was filled with plutonium.

"I'll explain," Balthazar grunted, then turned to Rose.

"You'll make the polenta," he said matter-of-factly. "Remember the polenta I showed you in Mexico? Just do that. You whisk cornmeal in a pot with boiling water. You add honey, then a sprig of rosemary, then you add—"

"The burp of the bloated bullfrog, I know," Rose said. "But we don't *have* the bloated bullfrog."

Lily must have overheard, because she hissed from across the aisle. "*Psst.* Rose. Do you mean *this* bloated bullfrog?"

Lily ducked behind her chopping block for a moment. When she stood back up, she was holding a blue mason jar – with the same uncomfortable amphibian Rose had met in Mexico leaning miserably against the side of the jar, holding his belly.

Rose could only stare, open-mouthed, as Lily laughed and tucked the jar back out of sight.

"You'd be so cool if you weren't so evil, *El Tiablo!*" Ty cried.

Rose turned to Balthazar, her eyes again filling with

tears. "Come here," he said quietly, putting his arm around her and turning her away from the ever-watchful cameras.

"You know I'm not one for sentimentality," he said into her ear. "But you. . . you're a good one, Rose. I've studied every recipe the Bliss family ever wrote, the life of every magical baker the Bliss family ever spawned, and you're one of the special ones. You could go on to invent great things. Today you're going to make the best darn polenta you ever made. Put love in it. That's the real magical ingredient, and you've got that in spades."

"But Lily. . . ," Rose said, struggling with her tears. "She. . ."

Balthazar shook his head. "No matter what happens today, I'm sorry to say that Lily will end up destroying herself. That kind of ambition has wrecked civilisations. You just stay good."

"So I just make the polenta without anything special in it?" Rose asked, wiping her nose with her sleeve.

Balthazar nodded. "That's right," he said. "And you know what? Things have a way of turning out special just when you need them to be."

Chapter 16

TEARS FROM A ROSE

As BALTHAZAR AND Rose went over the polenta recipe one more time, Jean-Pierre Jeanpierre re-entered the hall.

Balthazar gave Rose a kiss on the cheek and started back to the balcony as Jean-Pierre stepped up to the microphone on the cupcake stage. "You'll have one hour to bake," Jean-Pierre boomed. "Be bold. This is your final moment. As we say in Paris, *Bonne chance.*"

The massive baking timer on the wall began its ominous ticking, and Rose moved to her pantry shelf and began gathering what she'd need. Balthazar had stolen Ty away and was whispering to her brother about something or other, probably about how to mop Rose off the floor after losing turned her into a puddle of despair.

Rose was alone – no Booke, no magical ingredients. It felt like she was floating on her back in the middle of a vast indigo lake, her ears submerged in the water so that all she could hear was the sound of her own heartbeat. It was terrifying, floating in the middle of a lake by yourself; but there was still the sun, the clouds, the treetops. There was always something to grab on to.

So Rose picked up the box of cornmeal and a jar of honey, then put one foot in front of the other until she was standing in front of the stove. She measured one cup of water into a small saucepan, brought the water to boil, and added a half cup of the cornmeal, a sprig of rosemary, and two teaspoons of honey. As she stirred gently with a whisk, the tiny shards of dried corn began to swell and thicken into a golden-yellow porridge.

Rose felt one fat tear run down the length of her nose and then watched as it splashed into the cornmeal. When it hit the surface of the porridge, the tear made a curious spot of copper-coloured iridescence.

Was she wearing some sort of bronze mascara that she'd forgotten about? Why would a tear turn the cornmeal copper? But the spot quickly disappeared.

She continued to stand over the pot, stirring, as her tears plunked into the porridge, making tiny, copper-coloured explosions each time.

"Whoa, *mi hermana*! Those are some fat tears, man!"

Rose looked up from the saucepan and saw Ty standing next to her, his apron tied neatly around his waist.

He looked at the cornmeal on the stovetop. "How's it going? Looks good to me."

"I'm almost done, actually. But you can get a bowl."

Ty fished out three small bowls of red ceramic, and Rose ladled the polenta into the bowls, topping each with another sprig of rosemary. Together they arranged the bowls on the wooden chopping block, then stepped back and surveyed the scene. The bowls looked simple, rustic, and completely underwhelming.

From the stage, Jean-Pierre boomed, "Rosemary Bliss has finished with twenty minutes left on the clock, ladies and gentlemen! How brazen!"

"Well, Ty?" Rose laughed, relieved to be finished, even though what she'd finished was a failure. "What'll we do for twenty minutes?"

"I say we try to psych out *El Tiablo*."

They looked over at Lily's kitchen. Lily was stirring

a bowl of batter that flashed red, blue, or green, depending on how you looked at it.

"I feel like I've seen that batter before," said Ty. "But where. . ."

"Red, blue, green. . ." Suddenly Rose remembered seeing those alternating colours next to the multicoloured panels of a quilt during a backyard picnic months ago.

"The Hold-Your-Tongue Tart!" Rose hissed. "Remember when Lily made us that picnic in the backyard, and then she made us eat that tart—"

"She didn't have to make *me* eat it," Ty said. "That thing was *good.*"

"Yeah, but then we couldn't talk about what she was doing." Rose shook her head. "I don't like this. . ."

They watched as Lily took the box of her Secret Ingredient from the shelf and added a fistful of the chalky powder to the batter. An acrid, chemical stench wafted over from her kitchen, the same stench that Rose had smelled when she and Purdy had first tested the properties of the Secret Ingredient.

"That's it," murmured Rose. "The Hold-Your-Tongue Tart combined with Lily's Secret Ingredient. One will make Jean-Pierre think Lily is great, and the other will prevent him from talking about anything else he might taste, including our polenta. We're so toast."

"Nah, I'm still holding out hope," Ty said. "She's not even cooking with an unusual grain. She's completely ignoring the rules."

"You're right!" Rose said. "We might have a chance after all, if Jean-Pierre tastes ours first."

Lily pulled her tart from the oven. She finished arranging tiny leaves of mint on the top of her slice of tart just as the timer rang.

Jean-Pierre hobbled down the black-and-white aisle towards the two kitchens as an orchestra played a coronation march. In honour of the occasion, the master chef had donned a mink-lined red velvet cape with a three metre train, which Flaurabelle held out behind him.

He came to a stop between Rose and Lily, between the magical tart and the very ordinary polenta, and looked from side to side. "Which to taste first. . . ?" he mumbled to himself.

Rose dug her ragged, chewed nails into Ty's arm. He swatted her away. "Watch the dermis, *mujer*! I only get one!"

"I will perform a coin toss!" Jean-Pierre concluded. "Flaurabelle? The official coin, please!"

Flaurabelle pursed her red lips as she fished through her purse, ultimately pulling out a thin copper coin and handing it to Jean-Pierre.

Jean-Pierre turned to Lily. "I will let the older of the two finalists pick."

"Are you calling me *old*, Jean-Pierre?" Lily asked coyly.

"Ha-ha!" the master chef laughed. "Please pick a side, Ms Le Fay."

"Why, heads, of course!" She winked.

Jean-Pierre flipped the coin high in the air. "Whoever wins will have the first taste!"

The coin landed tails up.

"The tasting will commence in five minutes' time," proclaimed Jean-Pierre, consulting the timer.

"Hey," Sage said. The family had gathered in Rose's kitchen to await the final verdict. "Have either of you guys seen Gus? He wasn't around this morning, and he still hasn't shown up."

Rose shook her head no.

"I'm really worried about him," Sage went on. "He's my mentor."

"Hey!" Ty said. "I thought *I* was your mentor."

Sage beamed at his older brother. "You *did*?"

"Well, I, I mean, no," Ty said. "I suppose we haven't *officially* registered as mentor and protégé, but you're always free to observe my behavior and steal my tricks."

Ignoring Ty and Sage, Purdy folded Rose in her arms while Albert stroked her head. "You did great, honey," said Purdy.

"I didn't do great," Rose answered. "I didn't do much of anything. I made polenta."

"I bet it's really good, though. It looked real smooth. I didn't even need to dump these in," Ty said, holding up the vial of Rose's tears that Balthazar had handed to him earlier.

"She totally cried into it. Like, six big, fat tears at least."

"And did the polenta make a tiny copper explosion when the tears hit?" Balthazar asked.

Rose nodded, confused. What was all this about crying into the batter?

"Bang-o-rang!" Balthazar cried. "Tears of the pure at heart." Balthazar smiled. "I told Ty to add the tears, but I couldn't tell you what they were, Rose, because that would have spoiled them. Tears of the pure at heart are powerful things. Look at this."

Balthazar pulled a rumpled sheet of paper from his

back pocket and handed it to Rose. "I translated this while you were baking."

Tears of the Pure at Heart,
a Magical Additive to Any Baked Goode.
Tends to bring on a Miraculous Turn of Events.

It was in 1516, in the British town of Bristol, that the young Heather Bliss did engage in fierce battle with her foe, the wicked German warlord Maximilian Fronk. He did call a truce with the town leaders, but young Heather, suspicious of his intentions, did convince her twelve brothers to launch a surprise attack on Maximilian, wherein her eldest brother, Everett, was mortally wounded.

She did set to preparing his favorite porridge, to comfort him as he bled, and she cried into the pot. The tears stained the porridge a bright copper, and when Everett did eat of the bowl, his wounds closed.

Rose began to tear up again as she read the story of her ancestor Heather Bliss, who had tried desperately to protect her town and only ended up making things worse. How history does repeat itself.

But would Rose's tears be miraculous enough to override the powerful combination of a Hold-Your-Tongue Tart and Lily's Magic Ingredient?

Just then there was a crash and a scream from across the aisle.

"My mouse!" Lily cried. "That cat has stolen my mouse!"

Rose turned to find the birdcage atop Lily's pantry bookcase sitting empty, with the tiny door flung open. Gus stood in front of the cage, holding Jacques in his jaws.

"Gus!" Sage cried. "Don't eat him!"

Gus looked at Sage and winked, while Jacques gave them a cheerful thumbs-up. As Lily reached for a broom, Gus leaped to the ground and galloped down the room's centre aisle, disappearing through the doors just as Jean-Pierre strolled back in. Rose wouldn't have thought the fat cat could move so quickly.

"Jean-Pierre!" cried Lily. "Their earless cat stole my mouse!"

"Oh dear," Jean-Pierre said. "I suppose the cat was doing us all a favour, as mice have no place in a kitchen. But then again, neither do cats. Good riddance to the both of them!"

"But—" Lily protested.

"No buts," Jean-Pierre called as he made his way down the aisle. "Let's get the judging under way."

Chapter 17

CAUGHT ON TAPE

MARCO PLACED ROSE'S finished bowls of polenta on a silver tray as delicately as if they were baby chicks. He set Lily's slices of tart on another tray, then gently lifted each tray to his shoulders, one on each side. Carefully balancing the two, he turned and made his way down the black-and-white aisle to the stage.

Marco set the silver trays on a giant banquet table next to the microphone. Jean-Pierre sat down and draped a napkin over his chest, then picked up a knife and fork in his eager, sweaty fists. The master chef's eyes went wide with delight at the sight of Lily's shimmery Hold-Your-Tongue-Tart; they went wide with confusion at the sight of Rose's simple corn porridge.

"I will begin with Miss Bliss's dessert, as per our earlier coin toss," Jean-Pierre said. "Miss Bliss seems to have made. . . a bowl of yellow oatmeal." He dipped a spoon into Rose's bowl of polenta. "Will wonders never cease? I say, 'Make the most exquisite dessert the world has ever known,' and the child makes porridge! But, knowing her, it will probably manage to shake the earth, or something of that nature."

With great ceremony, the master chef lifted the spoonful of polenta and placed it in his mouth. He rolled the polenta around in his mouth thoughtfully, swallowed, then licked the spoon clean.

He closed his eyes and clutched at his heart. "I. . . I don't know what's happening to me. My heart is swelling." He peered at the empty spoon as it glinted in the harsh light of the cameras. "What have I just eaten?"

He took another hasty bite of the polenta, then another, and another, until finally he lifted the entire bowl to his mouth and slurped down everything that remained.

He set down the bowl, eyes closed, and sighed with contentment. "Ah, Miss Bliss," he said. "Another exquisite concoction."

Rose breathed a sigh of utter relief. The tears of the pure at heart might not be miraculous enough to best Lily's spiked Hold-Your-Tongue Tart, but they had managed to transform an ordinary bowl of cornmeal into something that Jean-Pierre found special. He looked down at Rose and smiled. "Will you tell me, what is your secret?"

Rose shrugged shyly, searching for a truthful answer to the question. She couldn't say "My tears were magic," of course, because there were at least ten cameras pointed at her face. The truth was that her secret was her family – not just the love and the support of her brothers and her sister and her parents, but her ancestors, and the whole matrix of ancient traditions and lessons that had been written down in the Booke. It was the powerful history of her family – that was her secret. That history meant everything to her, and she wanted it back.

"My family has been baking for a long time," she said, choking up. "For centuries. I'm just following in their footsteps."

Jean-Pierre winked at her. "Of course," he said. "I understand."

He turned his attention to Lily's tart, turning the plate round and round, mesmerised by the shimmering rainbow inside. "And now I'll taste Miss Le Fay's creation."

Jean-Pierre turned to the Hold-Your-Tongue Tart. The

tart couldn't prevent him from saying nice things about Rose's polenta, because he'd already said them, but the tart's magic was so powerful that it could make him forget he'd said any nice things at all.

Jean-Pierre gobbled a forkful of the tart. "Oh my," Jean-Pierre said, his eyes suddenly dead and dark, his voice robotic. "Oh, that's good. My, my, my. My, my, MY, my, my, that's good. The princess of pies has done it again. Unbelievable."

"Really?" Lily asked, clasping her hands together and pressing them to her chest. "I'm so glad!"

Rose glanced at her mother and rolled her eyes. Lily's Magic Ingredient had struck again.

Lily was standing with Jeremius across from Rose and her family. On the stage above them was the Gala's trophy, a silver whisk no less than seven feet high. There was a plaque at the base that read 78TH ANNUAL GALA DES GÂTEAUX GRANDS. GRAND PRIZE WINNER. MASTER OF THE BAKE.

Jean-Pierre put down his fork and leaned back, patting his rotund belly.

Lily batted her eyelashes at Jean-Pierre. "Well, don't stop eating *now*! There's so much more tart to love!"

"I have sampled enough to know that your tart is

the finest I have ever tasted," replied Jean-Pierre.

The master chef steepled his fingers together and stared off into the distance as he contemplated his decision. The hundreds of onlookers in the balconies above held their collective breaths in anticipation. Rose stared at the floor in despair. It seemed just one bite of the tart was powerful enough to win over Jean-Pierre. It wasn't fair. Lily was a liar and a cheater. But then again, Rose had done her fair share of lying and cheating that week as well.

Wasn't Lily's cheating much worse than Rose's, because she had started the whole thing? Or did it not really matter who started it?

Either way, the Bliss Cookery Booke was gone.

With a twirl of his moustache, Jean-Pierre stood and stepped to the microphone. "But the tart is not quite as fine as the polenta of Miss Rosemary Bliss! Miss Bliss is the winner of the seventy-eighth annual Gala des Gâteaux Grands!"

The crowd erupted in shouts and applause, but Rose was so dumbstruck by the master chef's announcement that she couldn't hear it. She felt like she was falling through a long tunnel, or rather soaring through it. She had won back the Booke, and she'd done it without cheating – she'd won with sincerity, the sincerity of her tears.

"Congratulations, *mi hermana!*" Ty said. He gave Rose a hug as their family crowded around them. Albert hoisted Rose on to his shoulders. "You did it!" he shouted. He paraded Rose around the expo centre as the spectators crowded the floor.

Blushing with embarrassment, unable to stop grinning, Rose looked back at her kitchen and saw Ty and Sage give each other high fives, while Purdy planted a kiss on Balthazar's withered cheek. Miriam and Muriel ran down from the balcony and planted one kiss on each of Ty's cheeks.

As Albert carried Rose above the cheering crowd, cameras followed her every move; hundreds of camera flashes flickered, but she ignored them all. She couldn't stop staring at the joy on her mother's face, the way her brothers were hugging each other, the way her father was prancing effortlessly around the room like he could carry her forever.

Rose looked over at Lily. Her aunt looked stunned, as if she couldn't believe what was happening any more than Rose could.

And Rose pitied her aunt for a moment. Rose had a

mother and a father and brothers and a sister and a great-great-great-grandfather who loved her – not to mention a devoted cat and a doting mouse. Even if Rose had lost, they would have been there for her. Lily had no one except for shrunken Jeremius, who at that moment was scowling at Lily and shaking his head. Lily had been paying people to love her, poisoning them into loving her, but now that she'd lost, she'd have to stop selling Lily's Magic Ingredient – at least according to the rules of the No-Renege Rugelach.

As Rose watched, Lily snapped back into 'performance mode.' She pasted on her signature smile and rushed over to Rose. She held up her hand, and Rose reached down and shook it.

"Congratulations!" Lily said. "Oh, you were *wonderful!*"

Rose climbed down from her father's shoulders as Ty hurried over. "All right, *El Tiablo,*" he said. "Cough it up!"

"Cough what up?" Lily asked innocently. She turned to the cameras with a laugh and shrugged.

"The Cookery Booke!" Sage cried. "That was the deal! We win, you give us the Booke!"

"That's right, you witch!" Miriam shouted. "Give them what's theirs!"

While Lily turned to say something to Jeremius, Sage pulled his tape recorder from his pocket and tucked it into the hood of Rose's sweatshirt.

"What are you doing?" said Rose.

"Trust me," he said, winking at his big sister.

Lily turned back to the Blisses. "Ohhhh, *that* Cookery Booke!" Addressing the cameras, she said, "I promised these children that if they won, I would give them an autographed copy of my family's old cookbook."

Lily held out her hand. Jeremius reached into a brocade satchel that hung over his shoulder and pulled out a thick tome covered in brown leather: the Bliss Cookery Booke.

Rose thought it was the most beautiful thing she'd ever seen. She took the Booke from Jeremius and held it close to her chest.

Lily put her arm around Rose and turned to face the cameras, her vast white smile glinting in the light. Smiling and nodding all the while, Lily bent and whispered in Rose's ear. "Enjoy it while you can, because I'm going to get the Booke back."

"*Steal* it back, you mean," Rose said.

"It's not *stealing*. I'm just doing what I have to do to get where I want to go. You don't seem to want to go anywhere. And that makes you a loser, Rose. You may have won the competition today, but you'll always be a loser."

"Can't you just be satisfied with your show?" Rose whispered. "You already got what you wanted. The whole world knows who you are now."

"It's not enough," Lily hissed through her smile. "It will never be enough."

Sage reached into the hood of Lily's sweatshirt and pulled out his tape recorder, then butted in between Rose and Lily. "What was that you were saying, Aunt Lily?" he asked, smiling at the cameras.

"I was telling her how impressed I was by her baking!" Lily said, also smiling for the cameras.

"Really?" Sage asked, rewinding the tape recorder. "'Cause I thought I heard you say *this*!"

Sage held the tape recorder up to the fuzzy grey microphone dangling overhead and pressed PLAY. "And that makes you a loser, Rose," piped Lily's voice through the tiny machine's speaker. "You may have won the competition today, but you'll always be a loser."

The crowd close enough to hear quieted in surprise; the cameramen looked up from their lenses in shock.

"I was joking!" Lily cried into the sudden quiet. "Doesn't

anyone understand sarcasm?" Lily turned to the cameras. "Folks watching at home, this young woman is wonderfully talented, and clearly a winner! I will even have her on my show if she would like! She could be my assistant!" Lily turned to Rose. "Would you like that?"

"No, thank you," said Rose.

A young reporter wearing a suit jacket that hung loosely around his skinny shoulders nudged Lily out of the way and spoke into the camera, one hand holding a microphone and the other pressing on his earpiece.

"Brent Highland, KRF News. This just in, viewers! Gala runner-up Lily Le Fay has officially been mean to adorable twelve-year-old winner Rosemary Bliss, telling her that she will, quote, 'Always be a loser.'"

Lily stared at the young reporter in horror, then sprang into action, tackling the reporter to the ground like a lion pouncing on a gazelle.

Two security guards shouldered through the crowd and seized Lily by the elbows. While Lily shrieked and batted at them, they dragged her through the crowd and out the doors of the expo centre, Jeremius running after them.

Rose reached down and helped the young reporter

to his feet. He brushed off the front of his jacket and picked up his microphone. "I'm here with the winner of the seventy-eighth annual Gala des Gâteaux Grands, and the youngest winner in Gala history: twelve-year-old Rosemary Bliss."

She took a deep breath and smiled into the camera. "Hello," she said.

"Now, Rosemary," said the reporter. "As young as you are, your victory might be a shock to some. Did you expect to win?"

"Absolutely not," Rose said. "There were more than a few times when I thought I was toast."

"Part of the surprise for Jean-Pierre Jeanpierre was the simplicity of your recipes," Brent continued. "Was this a deliberate strategy on your part?"

"Well, no," Rose said, thinking about it. "We just. . . we have some old family recipes that are simple, but very delicious."

"And where can viewers find these simply delicious recipes?" Brent asked.

Rose laughed. "I'm afraid they're going to have to remain a secret. But you can find them at the Follow Your Bliss Bakery in Calamity Falls, Indiana, or at La Panadería Bliss in Llano Grande, Mexico."

But the reporter was staring behind her. Rose turned to find Ty gazing into the camera, shifting between 'The Slow Burn' and 'The Sensitive Auto Mechanic.'

The reporter looked puzzled. "Is he all right?"

"Oh, he's fine," Rose said, putting her arm around Ty and dragging him forward. "This is my older brother, Thyme. He's not only the handsomest person I know, but also the most helpful."

Ty smiled sheepishly. "Thanks, *mi hermana*. You're not so bad yourself."

Sage was watching them from the side, staring with longing at the camera, so Rose reached over and pulled Sage into view. "And this is our younger brother, Sage, who is indispensable in a sticky situation."

"How did you like Paris, Sage?" Brent asked, holding out the microphone.

"I thought it was *Seine*-sational," Sage said with a wink. He took hold of the microphone. "But seriously, what a city. *Ei-ffel* in *Louvre* with it. There's nowhere in the uni-*Versailles* I would rather be."

Brent yanked his microphone back. "Puns! Funny! Rose, do you have any words for young aspiring bakers out there?"

Rose thought a minute. "Well, you ought to stick

with it, even after you mess up – but sticking with it is a lot easier if you have a family who believes in you."

Rose turned and beamed at her mother and father.

"And now, if you don't mind," she said, "we're all very hungry, and we're going to go eat lunch."

The cameramen and women put down their cameras and began packing up their equipment. Brent shook Rose's hand. "Great job, Miss Bliss. You're a natural."

"Natural is right!" The smell of cologne and tanning oil wafted out from behind the cameras as Joel and Kyle, the producers of *Lily's 30-Minute Magic*, leaned down to kiss the air on either side of Rose's cheeks.

"Wow," said Joel. "All I can say is, *W-O-W*. You were incredible out there!"

Without looking up from his mobile phone, Kyle said, "America loves you."

"What would you think of *Baking in Bliss?*" asked Joel.

"What's *Baking in Bliss?*" Rose asked, her head spinning from the smell of cologne.

"Your TV show, of course!" said Joel. "The future of *Lily's 30-Minute Magic* is uncertain – it was getting tired anyway. We're looking to fill the slot with something fantastic, something fresh, something completely unexpected, and that's you!"

My own TV show? Rose thought, stunned. What would she have to talk about on a TV show? She only knew about how to bake magical recipes in a small bakery.

"I don't know what to say," she answered truthfully. Of course being on TV would be exciting, but wouldn't it mean spending all her time away from her family, and the bakery? "I need to think about it, I guess," she said.

Joel shook Rose's hand. "Call us when you're ready to be a star."

Rose rejoined her family. Albert folded her into the huddle and patted her on the back. "Let's go drop the Cookery Booke off at the hotel," he said. "Then let's go stuff our faces."

Two hours later, Rose was stuffed to the brim with an early dinner of quiche lorraine and sole meunière and cassoulet. She and her siblings and her great-great-great-grandfather rode the elevator up to the family suite with the twins Desjardins. Purdy and Albert had stayed downstairs to check out of the Hôtel de Notre Dame and had sent Balthazar and the children ahead to pack their suitcases.

"I think I'm going to die," said Sage, stumbling along the carpeted hallway towards the Bliss family suite. "I've never eaten that much in my life. And I've eaten a lot in my life."

Ty said nothing – he just burped and patted his chest with his fist. "Excuse me, *amigas*," he said.

Miriam and Muriel stopped in front of their room. "Well," said Muriel, sighing. "I suppose this is goodbye."

Ty smoothed his hair. "Run on ahead, everyone. I've got to say goodbye to my new friends."

Everyone gave Miriam and Muriel hugs and two-cheeked kisses, then hurried down the hallway towards their room, leaving Ty to soak up one last glorious moment of romance.

Rose peeked back to see what Ty was up to. Would one of the impossibly glamorous Desjardins twins give her doofy older brother a kiss? Would both of them?

"You are wonderful, Ty," said Miriam.

"I agree," said Muriel. "You are a wonderful brother."

Ty hurriedly popped a piece of peppermint gum in his mouth, then stared, starry-eyed, at the twins.

"In fact, you remind us so much of our younger brother, Henri," said Miriam, "it's frightening. You look just like him. That is why we took such a liking to you."

"You are so cute – and so is he!" said Muriel. "We would know. We used to change his diapers."

"Looking at you is like looking at our little Henri, who we miss so much," said Miriam. "So thank you. Thank you for reminding us of our baby brother. And thank you for letting us be your big sisters this week."

Ty's face went from elated to bewildered to very depressed, all in a matter of seconds.

Rose would have smirked if she hadn't loved her brother so much.

"Thank you, I guess," he mumbled as the twins planted exaggerated, sisterly kisses on both of his cheeks.

Ty waved wanly, then turned and jogged towards the rest of his family.

"Sorry, brother," said Rose, patting him on the back. "You'll get 'em next time."

Rose caught up to Sage, Balthazar, and Leigh in front of the door to the Bliss family suite.

She opened the suite door and stepped into the darkened living room. She heard a rustling sound. "Jacques, is that you?"

"No!" he squeaked from her sweatshirt pocket. "I am right here, remember?"

Rose threw on the light switch.

Jeremius was hopping up and down on the ottoman, the Booke clutched to his chest. He cackled and once more leaped towards the open window.

Chapter 18

THE CAT WHO KICKED
THE HORNET'S NEST

"YOU GOTTA BE kidding me!" Ty cried. "We just spent a week getting that back!"

Gus launched himself from the baby sling on Balthazar's chest, leaped through the air like a caped action hero, and landed on Jeremius's head.

Jeremius reeled, confused, then finally swatted Gus across the room and clambered out the window. They watched Jeremius skip over to the adjacent rooftop and carry the Booke off into the afternoon.

"No!" Sage cried. He turned to Rose with tears in his eyes. "I'm sorry, Rose! You worked so hard!"

"Don't worry, Sage," said Rose, reaching into her backpack and pulling out a thick, dusty, brown leather-bound book. "The Booke is perfectly safe."

"Wait, that's. . . *that's* the Booke?" Sage gasped. "Then what did Jeremius steal just now?"

"The Shakespeare book I found in my room, the one we tried to trick him with earlier."

Sage and Ty exchanged a look, then Ty patted Rose on the back. "I'm impressed!" Ty said.

"What a great-great-great-granddaughter I have," Balthazar said proudly. "Out-tricking a professional trickster."

Meanwhile, the pile of grey fur on the ground was groaning. "Will no one help a Scottish Fold to his knees?" Gus cried.

Jacques crawled out of Rose's sweatshirt pocket, dropped to the ground, and darted over to where Gus lay, flat on his back, paws in the air. Jacques took hold of Gus's front paw and pulled with all his might, but the rotund cat wouldn't budge. Finally, Sage scooped him up and cradled him like a baby – a heavy, furry baby with yellow eyes.

Leigh flopped down on the couch. "Personally, I wish Lily had gotten away with the cookbook," she said, mimicking Rose's voice exactly. "She certainly would have done more with it."

Rose stared angrily at the Lily-loving demon who had occupied her little sister for far too long. "All right, Leigh. That's enough. I'm turning you back to normal, once and for all."

"I'd like to see you try," Leigh sneered at Rose using Rose's voice. "I am taking a nap, where I will dream of Lily's marvellous tart, which should have won the prize during today's festivities." Leigh rolled over to face the back of the couch and began, promptly, to snore.

"She must be stopped!" Gus shouted.

Rose plopped the Booke down on the granite kitchen counter and turned the pages. She loved the feel of them on her fingers: soft and worn, but strong, unbreakable.

She remembered what her mother had said months ago, after Leigh had eaten the tainted pound cake: "What she needs is—"

"—a Turn-Back Trifle," Balthazar piped in, finishing her sentence. Rose pawed through the pages, searching for the recipe.

"Why, when they assembled the Booke, did no one bother to put these in alphabetical order?" Rose huffed.

Finally, towards the middle of the Booke, Rose came upon the recipe:

Turn-Back Trifle,
for the Restoration of Time Lost.

It was in 1586, in the ill-fated colony of Roanoke, that Sir Lionel Bliss did construct this trifle for his beloved daughter Hatilda, whom he wished would stop growing up. The trifle did reverse Hatilda's age by one year for each layer of trifle she ate. Sir Bliss constructed a trifle of ten layers, and after taking a bite, poor Hatilda was again two years old.

"How is that going to help Leigh?" Sage asked. "If we make it two layers high, she'll disappear. Or she'll be in Mum's womb again or something. I don't think she would like that."

"A layer of trifle," Rose pontificated, "consists of sponge cake, fruit, custard, and whipped cream. So if we just give her the sponge cake, it'll turn her back a quarter of a year. Three months – right before she ate that poisoned pound cake."

Sir Lionel Bliss did begin his cake of sponge by placing two fists of FLOUR PURE AS SNOW in the centre of the wooden bowl. He cracked six of the CHICKEN'S EGGS

into the flour, then hovered over it with his mason jar,
releasing the STING OF THE ANCIENT HORNET.

"What the heck is an ancient hornet, *Abuelo*?" Ty asked.

"It's a hornet from the Queztmectal rain forests, destroyed by a fire in the fourteenth century. Their stingers had magical properties. There are only a few left in the world, and I have one. Or at least I did until that hateful little man ran off with my mason jars. We have no way of getting an ancient hornet."

Gus cleared his throat, accidentally coughing up a hair ball. "That's not necessarily true."

"What do you mean, Gus?" Balthazar asked suspiciously. "You weren't, say, rifling through my bags, were you?"

"I hate that hornet," Gus went on. "He used to say terrible things about me. Whenever I went near him, I could hear him chattering under his breath. 'Gus smells like tuna. Gus licks his own feet. Gus's tail makes him look like a bumper car.' One day I couldn't take it any more. I took the jar off the shelf, and I rolled it across the floor back and forth, like a hockey puck."

"I told you a million times not to do that!" Balthazar protested. "The hornet is hundreds of years old! He's delicate!"

"Sometimes I can't help myself," Gus replied. "Like the first day we arrived, for instance. I was passing by Balthazar's suitcase, and I heard his terrible little voice calling out for me, so I took him out of his jar and just. . . played hockey with him. I swatted him underneath the sink, but my paw couldn't reach in to fetch him out. He could still be there, but I don't know how we'll retrieve him. The space is too narrow."

"I shall go!" cried Jacques as he scampered over to the sink and darted into the tight space underneath.

A moment later he re-emerged, carrying the frail hornet in his paws. "You wouldn't believe how mean this hornet is! The things he said about me. . . I can't repeat them! He stings with his abdomen *and* with his words!" Jacques dumped the hornet into a little juice glass and wiped his hands clean.

"See?" sighed Gus.

While Rose mixed up the batter for the sponge cake, Balthazar looked through the pages of the Cookery Booke.

"What are you looking for?" Rose asked.

"Signs of misuse," he replied. "Missing pages, defamation, things like that."

Once Rose had finished the batter, she tilted the

juice glass in which the ancient hornet lay over the bowl. The hornet sighed as he slid to the rim of the glass. With a lot of creaking and complaining, he managed to stick his stinger into the yellow batter, which turned a violent, pulsing red. Rose tilted the glass away from the batter, and the hornet slid back to the bottom.

"Don't hornets die after they sting something?" Sage asked.

"Hornets do not die after stinging," Leigh piped in from the couch using Balthazar's deep, gravelly voice, "because their stingers are not barbed. Also, they are not *beetles*; they are part of the order Hymenoptera, whereas beetles are members of the order Coleoptera. I'm sure Lily knows all of the insect orders."

Ty turned to Rose. "Make the cake and feed it to her, *now*."

The rest of the sponge cake recipe was simple, and Rose rested the sheet of cake in the oven and set the timer for six songs.

After three songs, Purdy and Albert called up from the lobby to say that they were having some trouble checking out – something about the room bill – but that they'd be right back. Rose pulled the hot cake from the oven after the time of six songs, and she carried a slice over to Leigh.

"What is that?" she asked haughtily. "I don't want to eat it unless Lily made it."

Sage grabbed Leigh's shoulders and pinned her to the couch while Ty pried her mouth open.

"Unhand me, fools!" she cried.

Rose stuffed a few bites of the sponge cake into her sister's mouth, and Ty clamped Leigh's jaw shut until she had no choice but to chew and swallow.

They watched in wonder as Leigh's wild sprig of black hair seemed to pull back into her head about an inch and three months' worth of stains vanished from her *101 Dalmatians* T-shirt, leaving it only mildly browned and disgusting as opposed to abjectly browned and disgusting. The eerie black shimmer of her irises disappeared as her eyes slowly closed.

When Leigh opened them again, she giggled.

"Leigh?" said Rose, pinching Leigh's nose. "Do you know who Lily Le Fay is?"

Leigh put a tiny finger to her lips. "The bad one?"

"Right!" said Rose, hoisting her little sister up in her arms. "And do you know who I am?"

"Rosie!" she shrieked.

Rose buried her face in Leigh's dirty shirt. "I missed you, Leigh."

"Why? Where did I go?" she gurgled.

"Well, technically you didn't go anywhere. But I still missed you."

Jacques crawled up Rose's side and stared Leigh in the eye. "Wait. . . this child is not a demon sprite? She was merely under the spell of a witch?"

"Mousie!" Leigh cackled, grabbing at Jacques, who leaped from Rose's arm and landed between Gus's crumpled ears.

"Grandpa Balthazar," said Rose, "this is Leigh. The real Leigh."

"Nice to meet you," Balthazar grumbled, barely looking up from the Cookery Booke.

Just then, Purdy and Albert came through the doorway. Albert pointed at Rose and her brothers. "Are you all packed?"

"No," Rose answered. "But we got Leigh back to normal again!"

"You made the Turn-Back Trifle?" Purdy asked. "How many layers did she eat?"

"Just the sponge cake, Mum," Rose answered.

"Good girl," said Purdy. She looked Rose in the eye

as she pulled Leigh into her arms. "Rosie, you really are wonderful. I love you so much. And you too, Leigh!"

"Mama!" she cooed.

Balthazar looked up gravely. "Oh no," he said. "I was afraid of this."

"What?" Rose said, joining her grandfather at the counter.

"Look," he said, pointing to the hollowed-out compartment in the back cover of the book where Albatross's Apocrypha were stored. The collection of dangerous recipes was missing.

Instead, there was a tiny inscription written in Lily's flowery calligraphy.

Property of Lily Le Fay,
Novice
International Society of the Rolling Pin

"'Society of the Rolling Pin'?" Rose asked. "What's that?"

Balthazar sighed. "About a hundred years ago, Albatross descendants from all over the globe created a secret society. They've been working underground for years, creating all sorts of nastiness. Shrinking men with rotten milkshakes isn't even the half of it."

"What does that mean?" Rose squeaked.

"I suppose it means they'll be back for the Booke," he answered. "Not now, but sometime when you least expect it. You'll all have to be diligent." He paused. "You might even need a little. . . grandfatherly protection. I left my assistant Jorge in charge of my *panadería*. I don't think he'd mind running the place a little while longer. Besides, I think the cat has grown attached to you all."

"So it's just me that's grown attached, eh, old man?" Gus smirked from the couch, where he was tidying up his tail fur. "And you, as usual, feel nothing?"

"Of course," Balthazar growled.

"We've grown attached to you, too, *Abuelo*," said Ty, tousling what was left of his great-great-great-grandfather's hair.

Jacques hopped down from Gus's head and slumped off in the direction of the hole where they had first seen him. "And I suppose this is goodbye to Jacques."

Leigh scrambled down from Purdy's chest and waddled after Jacques.

"Come back, Mousie!"

Gus hopped down from the couch. "Jacques, whom I am proud to call my friend. You will join us as well.

That is, if the illustrious Mrs Bliss doesn't mind a mouse in the kitchen."

"Of course not," said Purdy.

Jacques stopped and pulled out his flute. "I have never been to America!" he exclaimed. "I must celebrate. Allow me to play the national anthem of America on my flute."

Everyone stood solemnly as Jacques piped out the strains of 'The Star-Spangled Banner.'

Rose knew that she had managed to recover the Booke and that she'd set Calamity Falls right again, all without any of Lily's cold, calculated magic. She had everything she needed right here: a passion for baking, a town she'd do anything to protect, and a family she loved. That was enough.

Rose stood with her family as each of them placed a hand over their hearts and listened to Jacques's hopeful tune.

ACKNOWLEDGMENTS

It was in 2011 in the City of New York that Kathryn Littlewood did pen this tome.

She did rely heavily upon the splendid creative genius of Ted Malawer and Michael Stearns at the Inkhouse to collect the story's ingredients. She did thereafter lean upon the inspired editorial guidance of Katherine Tegen and the Katherine Tegen Books family to trim the story's burnt edges and cover its entirety with a decadent frosting.

She did rely daily on the tender wisdom and creativity of her very own coven of magical women: Jocelyn, Laura Jean, Emily, and Alexandra.

When it was through, she did thank these wonderful individuals in the acknowledgments section of this book, because she would be hungry and lonely and quite bereft without them.

Also, she did watch the Food Network well, and often.

Don't miss the first book in
this delicious series!

'Quite delicious and very funny' *Wall Street Journal*

HarperCollins *Children's Books*